Risen From The Grave: Varney The Vampyre
Part Two:
The Flight Of The Vampyre
By James Malcom Rymer

Modernized by Leslie Ormandy

Scion Press
Oregon

Risen From The Grave: Varney The Vampyre
Part Two:
The Flight Of The Vampyre

Original Author: Malcom James Rymer
Modernization: Leslie Ormandy
Copyright © 2008, 2009 by Leslie Ormandy
Cover Art © 2008, 2009 by Sandy Ormandy

No part of this publication may be reproduced, stored in a retrieval system, or transmitted in any form or by any means, electronic, mechanical, photocopying, recording, or otherwise without prior written permission of the publisher.

Published in the USA.

Isbn – 13: 978-0-9822522-0-8
Isbn – 10: 0-9822522-0- X
Copyright # TXu 1-590-940

Lib of congress subject heading:
1. Vampire – Fiction
2. Serial – Fiction – Vampire
3. Gothic Romance - Fiction

Acknowledgments:

I owe thanks to many people. My daughter, Althea Infante, comes first, as always. She is closely followed by my sister, Sandy Ormandy, who is not only my sister but is my best friend as well. I believe it appropriate to thank Dr. Chang for giving me the huge gift of keeping me alive, often in spite of my whining. And I thank my second mom, Nancy Ormandy, for being an encourager in my life at all times. I have continually drawn the lucky-straw.

This book has seen the light of day only because of the loving assistance of my sister, Sandy Ormandy, who took the cover idea and ran with it, and my daughter, Althea Infante, who put up with the constant vampire conversations, and my father, Irvin Scott Ormandy, whose disapproval of my odd reading choices prompted me to claim that I was designing a class about Vampires. Then my Department Chair, Trista Cornelius, allowed my classes to become reality. These modernizations were prompted by students who simply couldn't handle the language – stilted and boring – and hence were shut out of the discussions.

I am a populist. No one should be shut out of a conversation by an elitist education system or an inability to read a language long since lexically shifted.

Preface:

Welcome back to the modernized, abridged version of *Varney the Vampyre*. As in the first volume, I have tried to ride the fine wire between producing a readable version, while leaving the tone, plot, and action of the original 1845 serialized version. Thus, as before, if the original words have no modern equivalents, you will find the definition in the footnotes.

"For the blood is the life."

Preface to Part Two:
by James Malcom Rymer

———

The unprecedented success of the gothic-romance "Varney the Vampyre" leaves the Author little to say other than that he accepts the success and its results gratefully.

A belief in the existence of Vampires first rose in Norway and Sweden, and it rapidly spread to more southern regions, taking a firm hold in the imaginations of the more gullible portion of mankind.

The following romance is collected from what seems the most authentic sources, and the author must leave the question of credibility entirely to his readers; not thinking that he is called upon to express his own opinion upon the subject.

Nothing has been omitted in the life of the unhappy Varney which could tend to throw a light upon his extraordinary life, and the fact of his death just as it is here related[1], made a great noise at the time through Europe, and is to be found in the public prints for the year 1713.

With these few observations, the author and publisher are content to leave the work in the hands of the public, which has stamped it with an appreciation far exceeding our most hopeful expectations, and which is calculated to act as the strongest possible incentive to the production of other works, which hopefully may be deserving of public patronage and support.

To the whole of the Metropolitan Press for their laudatory notices, the author is peculiarly obliged.

London Sep. 1847

The Flight Of The Vampyre

Chapter 44[ii]
Varney's Danger and His Rescue – The Prisoner Again – And the Subterranean Vault

The reader will remember the existence of a certain prisoner confined in a gloomy dungeon into which only the occasional and faint glimmering rays of light ever penetrate.

The prisoner is still there in his gloomy dungeon. He looks as though he is despairing, and his temples are still bound with the same cloths as before; they seem to have been soaked in crusty dried blood.

He still lives, although apparently incapable of movement. How he has survived is a mystery, for one would think him scarcely in a state, even were nourishment placed to his lips, to enable him to swallow it.

Occasionally a low groan bursts from his lips; it seems to come from the very bottom of his heart, and it sounds as if it would carry with it every remnant of vitality that was yet remaining to him.

Then he moves restlessly, and repeats in hurried accents the names of some who are dear to him, and far away – some who may, perhaps, be mourning him.

As he moves, the rustle of a chain against the straw on which he lies gives an indication that even in this abandoned dungeon it has not been considered prudent to leave him master of his own actions, lest, by too vigorous an effort, he might escape from the prison in which he is held.

A sound reaches his ears, and for a few moments, in the deep impatience of his wounded spirit, he heaps curses on the heads of those who have reduced him to his present state. But soon a better nature seems to come over him, and gentler words fall from his lips. He preaches patience to himself; he does not talk of revenge, but of justice, and with more hopefulness than he had before spoken, he calls upon Heaven to aid him in his deep distress. Then all noise is still, and the prisoner appears to resign himself once more to the calmness of expectation, or of despair, but listen! His sense of hearing, rendered doubly acute by lying so long alone in near darkness and silence, detects sounds which to ordinary mortal powers of perception would have been too indistinct to be heard.

It is the sound of feet far overhead; he hears them. They beat the green earth – that sweet, green earth which he may never see again – with an impatient tread. They come on…nearer and still nearer, and

The Flight Of The Vampyre

now they pause; he listens with all the intensity of one who listens for existence. Someone comes; there is a lumbering noise – a hasty footstep; he hears someone laboring for breath – panting like a hunted hare. His door is opened, and a man staggers in, tall and gaunt; he moves like one intoxicated, yet fatigue has done more than the work of inebriation; he cannot save himself, and he sinks exhausted by the side of that lonely prisoner.

The captive raises himself as far as his chains will allow him; he clutches the throat of his enervated visitor.

"Villain, monster, vampyre!" he shrieks, "I have you now," and locked in a deadly embrace they roll upon the damp earth, each struggling for life.

*****

It is midday at Bannerworth Hall, and Flora is looking from the casement anxiously, expecting the arrival of her brothers. She had seen from some of the topmost windows of the Hall that the whole neighborhood has been in a state of commotion, but little does she guess the cause of so much tumult, or think that it in any way might concern her.

She had seen the local villagers forsaking their work in the fields and the gardens, but she feared to leave the house. She had promised Henry that she would not leave in case the promised peaceful conduct of the vampyre had been a trick to draw her away from her home to lead her into some danger. Yet more than once she was tempted to forget her promise and to seek the open country. She feared that those she loved could be encountering some danger for her sake which she would willingly either share with them, or spare them.

The promise she had made to her brother kept her comparatively quiet; moreover, since her last interview with Varney in which he had shown some feeling for the melancholy situation to which he had reduced her, she had been more able to reason calmly, and to meet the suggestions of passion and of impulse with a sober judgment.

About midday she saw the domestic party returning – that party which now consisted of her two brothers, the Admiral, Jack Pringle, and Mr. Chillingworth. As for Mr. Marchdale, he had given them a polite farewell on the confines of the grounds of Bannerworth Hall, stating that although he had felt it to be his duty to come forward and second Henry Bannerworth in the duel with the vampyre, yet that circumstance by no means obliterated from his memory the insults he had received from Admiral Bell and; therefore, he declined going to Bannerworth Hall, and bade them instead a very good morning.

To all this, Admiral Bell replied that he might leave and be damned, and that he considered him a swab and a humbug, and he appealed to Jack Pringle whether he, Jack, ever saw such a sanctified looking prig[iii] in his life.

"Ay, ay," Jack answered.

This answer produced the usual contention, which lasted them until they got inside the house, where they swore at each other to an extent that was enough to make anyone's hair stand on end; Henry and Mr. Chillingworth intervened, begging them to postpone the discussion until some more fitting opportunity.

Everything which had occurred was then related to Flora; who, while she blamed her brother for fighting the duel with the vampyre, found in the conduct of that mysterious individual– at least regarding this encounter – yet another reason for believing him to be strictly sincere in his desire to save her from the consequences of his future visits.

Her desire to leave Bannerworth Hall became more and more intense, and since the Admiral now considered himself the master of the house, they offered no opposition to the idea of leaving, but merely said, "My dear Flora, Admiral Bell shall decide all these matters now. Whatever he says we ought to do, we shall do; he will be dictated by the best possible feelings towards us."

"Then I appeal to you, sir," said Flora, turning to the Admiral. "I would like to leave this place where there are so many evil occurrences and memories."

"Very good," replied the old man; "then I say..."

"Nay, Admiral," interrupted Mr. Chillingworth; "you promised me only a short time ago that you would come to no decision upon this question until you had heard some details which I have to relate to you. In my humble opinion, they will sway your judgment."

"I had forgotten all about it, but I did indeed agree with your request," the Admiral said. "Flora, my dear, I'll be with you in an hour or two. My friend, the good doctor here, has got some idea, and fancies it's the right one; however, I'll hear what he has got to say first, before we come to a conclusion. So come along Mr. Chillingworth, and let's have it out at once."

"Flora," said Henry, when the Admiral had left the room with Mr. Chillingworth, "I know that you wish to leave the Hall. Your wishes will go far in our considerations."

"I do wish to depart, but not to go far. I wish rather to hide from Varney than to make myself inaccessible to him by distance."

"You want to remain in this neighborhood?"

"I do, and you know with what hope I cling to it."

"Perfectly; you still think it possible that Charles Holland may be united to you."

"I do."

"You believe his faithfulness."

"Oh, yes; as I believe in Heaven's mercy."

"And I, Flora; I would not doubt him now for worlds. I have come to believe in his honesty as greatly as you."

"Oh yes, Henry," Flora exclaimed enthusiastically; "this may be only some trial, grievous while it lasts, but yet tending eventually only to make the future look more bright and beautiful. Heaven may yet have in store some great happiness which shall spring clearly and decidedly out of these misfortunes."

"It may be so, and may we always banish despair by such hopeful beliefs. Lean on my arm, Flora; you are safe with me. Come, dearest, let me take you to the garden and let the sweetness of the morning air refresh you."

There was a new hopefulness about the manner in which Henry Bannerworth spoke, such as Flora had not for many weary months had the pleasure of listening to, and she eagerly rose to accompany him into the garden. It was glowing with all the beauty of sunshine, for the day had turned out to be much finer than the early morning had hinted it would be.

"Flora," he said, when they had walked to and fro in the garden for awhile, "notwithstanding all that has happened, there is no convincing Mr. Chillingworth that Sir Francis Varney is really what he appears to us."

"There is not?"

"It is so. In the face of all evidence, he will neither believe in vampyres at all, nor that Varney is anything but some mortal man, like ourselves, in his thoughts, talents, feelings, and modes of life, and with no more power to do anyone an injury than we have."

"Oh, I wish that I could think so!"

"And I. But unhappily we have far too many evidences to the contrary. And though, while we respect the strength of mind in our friend which not allow him, even almost at the last extremity, to yield to what appear to us to be stern facts, we may not ourselves be so obdurate[iv], but may feel that we know enough to be convinced."

"You have no doubt that Varney is the Vampyre, brother?"

"Most reluctantly, I must confess, I feel compelled to consider Varney as something more than mortal."

"He must be so."

"And now, sister, before we leave the place which has been a home to us from earliest life, let us for a few moments consider if there is any possible proofs supporting the idea of Mr. Chillingworth; that Sir Francis Varney wants possession of the house for some purpose more hostile to our peace and prosperity than any he has yet attempted."

"He holds such an opinion?"

"He does."

"It seems very strange."

"He seems to gather from all the circumstances which have recently occurred that Sir Francis Varney has an overwhelming desire to become the tenant of Bannerworth Hall."

"Varney certainly does wish to possess it."

"Yes, but can you, sister, in the exercise of any possible amount of fancy, imagine any motive on the part of Varney for such an anxiety beyond what he alleges?"

"Which is merely that he is fond of old houses, and ours being such a nice example of old house, he wishes to possess it?"

"Precisely. That is the reason he states, and the only one that can be got from him. Heaven only knows if it is the true one."

"It may be true, brother."

"As you say, it may, but there is a doubt nevertheless. Flora, I much rejoice that you have had an interview with this mysterious being, for you have certainly, since that time, been happier and more composed than I ever hoped to see you again."

"I have indeed felt happier since that interview. I have not had the same sort of dread of Sir Francis Varney which before made the very sound of his name a note of terror to me. His words and all he said to me during that interview which took place so strangely between us, tended to make him, to a certain extent, an object of my sympathies rather than my distaste."

"That is very strange."

"I can agree that it is strange, Henry, but when we come for but a brief moment to reflect upon the circumstances which have occurred, we shall, I think, be able to find cause to pity Varney the vampyre."

"How?"

"Thus, brother. It is said that those who have been once subject to the attack of a vampyre are themselves to become one of the dreadful and terrible creatures."

"I confess that I have heard the same," replied Henry, seating her beside him on a likely bench.

"Yes, and therefore who knows but that Sir Francis Varney may, at one time, have been as innocent as we are ourselves of the terrible and fiendish propensity which now makes him a terror and a reproach to all who know him, or are in any way subjected to his attacks."

"That is true."

"There may have been a time – who shall say there was not – when he, like me, would have shrunk with a dread as great as anyone could have experienced from the contamination of even the touch of a vampyre."

"I cannot, sister, deny the soundness of your reasoning," Henry said with a sigh; "but still I do not see anything, even with a full conviction that Varney is unfortunate, which should induce us to tolerate him."

"Nay, brother, I did not say, 'tolerate.' What I mean is this, that even with the horror and dread we must naturally feel at such a being, we may yet mingle some amount of pity, which shall make us rather seek to shun him, than to cross his path with a resolution of doing him an injury."

"I perceive well what you mean. Rather than remain here making an attempt to defy Sir Francis Varney, you would fly from him, and leave him undisputed master of the field."

"I would!" She agreed strongly; "I would."

"Heaven forbid that anything would thwart you. You know how dear you are to me; you know very well that your happiness has always been a matter which has assumed the most important of shapes. It is not likely, dearest sister that we should thwart you in your wish to get away from here."

"I know, Henry, all you would say," remarked Flora as tears started in her eyes. "I know very well your thoughts, and indeed, your love for me, I likewise know I may rely on you forever. I know how you are attached to this place, as we all are, by a thousand pleasant associations, but listen to me further, Henry; I do not wish to wander far from this place."

"Not far, Flora?"

"No. As I said before, I still cling to a hope that Charles may yet appear. And if he does so, it will assuredly be in this neighborhood, which he knows is our home and most dear to us all."

"What you have said is true."

"Then understand that what I wish is to make some sort of public, departure of our leaving the Hall. And yet I do not wish to go far. In the neighboring town, for example, surely we might find some means of living entirely free from remark or observation as to who or what we were."

"That, sister, I doubt," Henry remarked dryly, acutely aware of his recent experience with the rectitude of servants, and the speed with which news traveled. "If you seek for that species of solitude which you contemplate, it is only to be found in a desert or in a large city."

"Indeed?" she asked in tones of puzzlement.

"Ay, Flora; you may well believe me, that it is so. In a small community you can have no possible chance of evading an amount of scrutiny which would very soon pierce through any disguise you could by any possibility assume."

"Then there is no other choice," she muttered in new despair, "we must go far."

"Nay, I will consider your wishes, Flora, and although, as a general principle, what I have said I know to be true, yet we might yet find some means, for Charles Holland's sake, of remaining in this immediate neighborhood, that will yet procure to us all the secrecy we may desire."

"Dear – dear brother," said Flora, flinging herself upon Henry's neck, "you speak cheeringly to me, and what is more, you believe in Charles's faithfulness and truth."

"As Heaven is my judge, I do."

"A thousand, thousand thanks for such an assurance. I know him too well to doubt for one moment, his faith. Oh, brother! could he – could Charles Holland, the soul of honor, the abode of every noble impulse that can adorn humanity – could he have written those letters? No, no! perish the thought!"

"I only wonder how I could ever have suspected him of such disloyalty," Henry exclaimed

"It is very generous of you to say so, dear brother, but you know as well as I that there has been someone here who has taken the worst view of Charles's mysterious disappearance, and attempted to induce us to believe the same."

"You allude to Mr. Marchdale?"

She nodded.

"Well, Flora, I must admit you have cause for speaking of Mr. Marchdale as you do, yet when we come to consider all things, excuses may be found for his opinions."

"May there be?" she sputtered.

"Yes, Flora; he is a man past the meridian of life, and the world is a sad as well as a bad teacher, for it soon deprives us of our trusting confidence in human nature."

"That may be so, and I will acknowledge out of fairness that he knows very little of Charles Holland, yet still he judged him hastily and harshly."

"It would be kinder to say, Flora, that he did not judge him generously. And you must recollect that Mr. Marchdale did not like Charles Holland."

With a quick change of topic she pointed suddenly, "Look yonder!"

"Where?"

"There. Do you see the Admiral and Mr. Chillingworth walking among the trees?"

"Yes, yes; I do."

"How very serious and intent they are upon the subject of their discourse. They seem quite lost to all surrounding objects. I could not have imagined any subject than would so completely have absorbed the attention of Admiral Bell."

"Mr. Chillingworth had something to relate to him of a nature which, perchance, has had the effect of capturing all his attention – he called him from the room."

"Yes; I saw that he did. But see, they now come towards us, and now we shall hear the subject-matter of their discourse and consultation."

Admiral Bell had evidently seen Henry and his sister where they were sitting in the shaded garden, for now he broke off his private discourse with Mr. Chillingworth as if they arrived at some point in it which enabled them to come to a conclusion to be communicated. They now turned their steps towards the brother and sister.

"Well," shouted the bluff old Admiral when they were sufficiently near to exchange words, "well, Miss Flora, you are looking a thousand times better than you were."

"Thank you, Admiral, I am feeling much better."

"To be sure you are, and you will be much better still, and no sort of mistake. Now, here's the doctor, and he and I have both been agreeing upon what is best for you."

"You have?" she faltered.

"Yes, to be sure. Have we not, Doctor?"

"We have, Admiral."

"Good, and what, now, Miss Flora, do you suppose we have decided?"

"I really cannot say."

"Why, it's a change of air, to be sure. You must get away from here as quickly as you can, or there will be no peace for you."

"Yes," added Mr. Chillingworth, advancing; "I am quite convinced that a change of scene will tend more to your recovery than any other circumstances. In the most ordinary cases of indisposition we always find that the invalid recovers much sooner away from the scene of his indisposition, than by remaining in it."

"Well said," said the Admiral.

"Then we are to understand," said Henry with a smile, "that we are no longer to be your guests, Admiral Bell?"

"Hold up there!" cried the Admiral; "who told you to understand any such thing, I should like to know?"

"Well, we shall look upon this house as yours, now, and that being the case, if we remove from it, of course we cease to be your guests any longer."

"That's all you know about it. Now, listen to me. You don't command the fleet, so don't pretend to know what the Admiral is going to do." The listeners allowed that they would listen quietly to the Admiral's instructions.

"I have decided that I am going to invest my spare cash in taking houses; so, as I don't care at all where the houses may be situated, you can look out for one somewhere that will suit you, and I'll take it; so, after all, you will be my guests there just the same as you are here."

"Admiral," protested Henry, "it would be imposing upon a generosity as rare as it is noble were we to allow you to do for us what you contemplate."

"But I say you shall. So you have had your say, and I have had mine. If you please, Master Henry Bannerworth, I shall take upon myself to consider the affair as altogether settled. You can commence operations as soon as you like. I know that Miss Flora, here – bless her sweet eyes – don't want to stay at Bannerworth Hall any longer than she can help it."

"Indeed I was urging upon Henry to remove from this place," said Flora; "but yet I cannot help feeling with him, Admiral, that we are imposing upon your goodness."

"Go on imposing, then."

"But... "

"Psha! Can't a man be imposed upon if he likes? Damn it; that's a poor privilege for an Englishman to be forced to make a row about. I tell you I like it. I will be imposed upon, so there's an end of that, and now let's come in and see what Mrs. Bannerworth has got ready for lunch."

* * * * * *

It can hardly be supposed that such a popular ferment as had been created by the singular reports concerning Varney the vampyre, should readily, and without abundant satisfaction, subside.

Mobs do not reason very clearly, but the fact of the frantic flight of Sir Francis Varney from the projected attack of the infuriated multitude was seized hold of as positive proof of the reality of his vampyre-like existence. Then, again, had he not disappeared in the most mysterious manner? Had he not sought refuge where no human being would think of seeking refuge, namely in that old, dilapidated ruin, where when his pursuers were so close upon his track, he had succeed in eluding their grasp with an ease which made it look as if he had vanished into thin air, or as if the very earth had opened to receive him bodily within its cold embraces?

The few who fled so quickly from the ruin lost nothing of the wonderful story they had to tell while carrying it from that place to the town. When they reached their neighbors, they not only told what had really occurred, but they added to it all their own surmises and the fanciful creation of all their own fears, so that before mid-day, and about the time when Henry Bannerworth was conversing so quietly in the gardens of the Hall with his beautiful sister, there was an amount of popular ferment in the town of which they had no conception. All business was suspended. Many persons, now that the idea had been started concerning the possibility that a vampyre might have been visiting some of the houses in the place, were quick to tell how, in the dead of the night, they had heard strange noises. How children had shrieked from no apparent cause, doors opened and shut without human agency, and windows rattled that never had been known to rattle before.

Some went so far as to declare that they had been awakened out of their sleep by noises, telling of an effort being made to enter their chambers while others had seen dusky forms of gigantic proportions outside their windows, tampering with the window fastenings, and only disappearing when the light of day mocked all attempts at concealment.

These tales flew from mouth to mouth, and all listened to them with such an eager interest that none thought it worthwhile to challenge their inconsistencies, or to express a doubt of their truth because the stories had not been mentioned before.

The only individual, and he was a remarkably clever man, made the slightest remark upon the subject of a practical character; he hazarded a suggestion that made confusion worse instead of better.

He knew something about vampyres. He had travelled abroad, and he had heard of them in Germany as well as in the east, and to a crowd of wondering and aghast listeners, he said, "You may depend upon it, my friends, this has been going on for some time; there have been several mysterious and sudden deaths in the town lately; people have wasted away and died."

"Yes – yes," said everybody.

"There was Miles, the butcher; you know how fat was – and then how fat he wasn't."

A general assent was given to the proposition, and then, elevating one arm, the clever fellow continued, "I have no doubt that Miles, the butcher, and everyone else who has died suddenly lately have been victims of the vampyre, and what's more, they'll all be vampyres and come and suck other people's blood, till at last the whole town will be a town of vampyres."

"But what's to be done?" cried one, trembling so excessively that he could scarcely stand under his apprehension.

"There is only one possible plan: Sir Francis Varney must be found and put out of the world in such a manner that he can't come back to it again, and all those who are dead that we have any suspicion of should be taken up out of their graves and looked at to see if they're rotting or not; if they are then it's all right, but if they look fresh and much as usual, you may depend they're vampyres and no mistake."

This was a terrible suggestion thrown amongst a mob. To have caught Sir Francis Varney and immolated[v] him at the shrine of popular fury, they would not have shrunk from, but a desecration of the graves of those whom they had known in life was a matter which, however much it had to recommend it, even the boldest stood aghast at, and felt some qualms of irresolution. There are many ideas which, like the first plunge into a cold bath, are rather uncomfortable for the moment, but which, in a little time, we become so familiarized with that they become stripped of their disagreeableness and appear quite pleasing and natural.

So in was with this notion of exhuming the dead bodies of those townspeople who had recently died from what was called a decay of nature, and such other failures of vitality as bore not the tangible name of any understood disease.

From mouth to mouth the awful suggestion spread like wildfire, until at last it grew into such a shape that it almost seemed to become a duty, at all events, to have up Miles the butcher and see how he looked. There is, too, about human nature a natural craving curiosity concerning everything connected with the dead. There is not a man of education or of intellectual endowment who would not travel many miles to look upon the exhumation of the remains of someone famous in his time, whether for his vices, his virtues, his knowledge, his talents, or his heroism, and if this feeling exists in the minds of the educated and refined in a sublimated shape, we may look for it among the vulgar and the ignorant, taking only a grosser and meaner form in accordance with their habits of thought. And so this vulgar curiosity combined with other feelings, prompted an ignorant and illiterate mob to exhume Miles.

And it was wonderful to see how, when these people had made up their minds to carry out the singularly interesting, but at the same time fearful, suggestion, they assumed to themselves a great virtue in doing it. They told each other what an absolute necessity there was; it was for the public good that it should be done, and then, with loud shouts and cries concerning the vampyre, they proceeded in a body to the village church-yard, where had been lain, with a hope of reposing in peace, the bones of their ancestors.

A species of savage ferocity now appeared to have seized upon the crowd, and the people, in making up their minds to do something which was strikingly at variance with all their preconceived notions of right and wrong, appeared to feel that it was necessary, in order that they might be consistent, to cast off many of the decencies of life, and to become riotous and reckless. As they proceeded toward the graveyard, they amused themselves by breaking the windows of the tax-gatherers, and doing what passing mischief they could to the habitations of all who held any official situation or authority.

This was something like a proclamation of war against those who might think it was their duty to interfere with the lawless proceedings of an ignorant multitude. A tavern or two, likewise in the path of the multitude, were sacked of some of the inebriating contents; so that, what with the madness of intoxication and the general excitement consequent upon the very nature of the business which took them to the churchyard, a more wild and infuriated multitude than that which paused at two iron gates which led into the sanctuary of that church, could not be imagined.

Those who have never seen a mob that has cast off all moral restraints can form no notion of the mass of terrible passions which lie slumbering under what, in ordinary cases, have appeared harmless bosoms – but which now run riot and overcome every principle of restraint. It is a melancholy fact, but nevertheless a fact despite its melancholy, that even in a civilized country like this, with a generally well-educated population, nothing but a well-organized physical force keeps hundreds and thousands of persons from the commission of outrageous offenses. In this case the there is no physical power that could cope with the mob's intent.

We have said that the mob paused at the iron gates of the churchyard because they saw that those iron gates were closed. This had not been the case within the memory of the oldest among them.

When the church and the graveyard were first built, two pairs of these massive gates had been presented by some munificent patron, but after a time the gates hung idly upon their hinges, ornamental certainly, but useless.

But now those strong ornamental gates were closed, for once doing their duty. Heaven only knows how they had been moved upon their rusty and time-worn hinges. The mob, however, was checked for the moment, and it was clear that the ecclesiastical authorities were resolved to attempt something to prevent the desecration of the tombs.

Those gates were sufficiently strong to resist the first vigorous shake which was given to them by some of those among the forefront of the crowd, and then one fellow suggested the idea that they might be opened from the inside, and volunteered to clamber over the wall to do so.

Hoisted up upon the shoulders of several, he grasped the top of the wall and raised his head above its level; something of a mysterious nature then rose up from the inside, dealing him such a whack between the eyes that down he went sprawling among his compatriots. Now, nobody had seen how this injury had been inflicted, and the policy of those holding the graveyard should have certainly been to keep up the mystery, leaving the invaders in ignorance of what sort of person it was that had so foiled them. Man, however, is prone to indulge in vain glorification, and the secret was exploded by the triumphant waving of the long staff of the Beadle[vi], with the gilt knob at the end of it, just over the parapet of the wall in token of victory.

"It's Waggles! It's Waggles!" cried everybody; "it's Waggles, the Beadle!"

"Yes," said a voice from within, "it's Waggles, the beadle, and he thinks as he had you there; try it again. The church isn't in danger; oh, no. What do you think of this?" The staff was flourished more vigorously than ever, and in the secure position that Waggles occupied it seemed not only impossible to attack him, but that he possessed wonderful powers of resistance, for the staff was long and the knob was heavy.

It was a boy who hit upon the ingenious expedient of throwing up a great stone, so that it just fell inside the wall, and hit Waggles a great blow on the head.

The staff was then flourished more vigorously than ever, and the mob, in ecstasy of the fun which was going on, almost forgot the errand which had brought them to the graveyard. Perhaps, after all, the affair might have passed off jestingly, had there not been some really mischievous persons among the throng who were determined that such should not be the case, and they incited the multitude to commence an attack upon the gates, which in a few moments, must have produced their entire demolition.

Suddenly, however, the boldest drew back, and there was a pause as the well-known form of the clergyman appeared advancing from the church door, attired in his official outfit.

"There's Mr. Leigh," said several; "how unlucky that he should be here."

"What is this?" asked the clergyman approaching the gates. "Can I believe my eyes when I see before me those who compose the worshippers at this church, armed, and attempting to enter for the purpose of violence to this sacred place! Oh! let me beseech you, lose not a moment but return to your homes and repent of that which you have already done. It is not yet too late; listen, I pray you, to the voice of one with whom you have so often joined in prayer to the throne of the Almighty, who is now looking upon your actions."

This appeal was heard respectfully, but it was evidently very far from suiting the feelings and the wishes of those to whom it was addressed; the presence of the clergyman was evidently an unexpected circumstance, and the more especially too as he appeared in that costume which they had been accustomed to regard with a reverence almost amounting to veneration. He saw the favorable effect he had produced, and anxious to follow it up, he added, "Let this little impulse of feeling pass away, my friends, and believe me when I assure you upon my sacred word, that whatever ground there may be for complaint or subject for inquiry, shall be fully and fairly met, and that the greatest exertions shall be made to restore peace and tranquility to all of you."

"It's all about the vampyre!" cried one fellow. "Mr. Leigh, how should you like a vampyre in the pulpit?"

"Hush, hush! can it be possible that you know so little of the works of that great Being whom you all pretend to adore, as to believe that he would create any class of beings of a nature such as those you ascribe to that terrible word? Oh, let me pray of you to get rid of these superstitions – alike disgraceful to yourselves and afflicting to me."

The clergyman had the satisfaction of seeing the crowd rapidly thinning from in front of the gates, and he believed his exhortations were having all the effect he wished. It was not until he heard a loud shout behind him, and upon hastily turning, that he saw that the churchyard had been scaled at another place by some fifty or sixty persons. His heart sank within him, and he began to feel that what he had dreaded would surely come to pass.

Even then he might have done something in the way of peaceful exertion, but for the interference of Waggles, the Beadle, who spoilt everything.

Chapter 45
The Open Graves – The Dead Bodies – A Scene of Terror

We have said Waggles spoilt everything, and so he did, for before Mr. Leigh could utter a word more, or advance a few steps towards the rioters, Waggles charged them staff in hand, and there soon ensued a riot of a most formidable description.

A kind of desperation seemed to have seized the Beadle, and certainly his sudden and unexpected attack achieved wonders. When, however, a dozen hands got hold of the staff, and it was wrenched from him, and he was knocked down, and half-a-dozen people rolled over him, Waggles was not nearly the same man he had been, and he would have been very content to have lain quiet where he was. He was not permitted to do this, for two or three who had felt what a weighty instrument of warfare a parochial staff was, lifted him bodily from the ground and tossed him over the wall, without much regard to whether he fell on a hard or a soft place on the other side.

This feat completed, no further attention was paid to Mr. Leigh, who, upon finding that his exhortations were quite unheeded, retired into the church with an appearance of deep affliction about him, and he locked himself in the vestry.

The crowd now had possession of the burial-ground, and soon in a dense mass these desperate and excited people collected round the well-known spot where the mortal remains of Miles, the butcher, resided in peace.

"Silence!" cried a loud voice, and everyone obeyed the mandate, looking towards the speaker, who was a tall, gaunt-looking man, attired in a suit of faded black, and who now pressed forward to the front of the throng.

"Oh!" cried one; "it's Fletcher, the Ranter[vii]. What does he want here?"

"Hear him! Hear him!" cried others; "he won't stop us."

"Yes, hear him," cried the tall man, waving his arms about like the sails of a windmill. "Yes, hear him. Sons of darkness; you're all vampyres and are continually sucking the life-blood from each other. No wonder that the evil one has power over you all. You're as men who walk in the darkness when the sunlight invites you, and you listen often to the words of humanity when those of a more divine origin are offered to your acceptance. But there shall be miracles in the land, and even in this place, set apart with a pretended piety that is in itself most damnable, you shall find an evidence of the true light, and the proof that those who will follow the true path to glory shall be found here within this grave. Dig up Miles, the butcher!"

There was a general shout of appreciation at this instruction. And several told each other loudly, "Mr. Fletcher's not such a fool, after all. He means well."

"Yes, you sinners," said the Ranter, "and if you find Miles, the butcher, decaying – even as men are expected to decay whose mortal tabernacles are placed within the bowels of the earth – you shall gather from that a great omen, and a sign that if you follow me you seek the Lord, but if you find him looking fresh and healthy, as if the warm blood was still within his veins, you shall take that likewise as a signification that what I say to you shall be as the Gospel, and that by coming to the chapel of the Little Boozlehum[viii], ye shall achieve great salvation."

"Very good," said a brawny fellow, advancing with a spade in his hand; "you get out of the way, and I'll soon have him up. Here goes like blue blazes!"

He cast the first shovelful of earth he took up over his head into the air, so that it fell in a shower among the mob, which of course raised a shout of indignation. As he continued to dispose of the superfluous earth in this manner, a general quarrel seemed likely to ensue. Mr. Fletcher opened his mouth to make a remark, and as that feature of his face was rather a large one, a descending lump of earth fell into it and got so wedged among his teeth, that in the process of extracting it he nearly brought those essential portions of his anatomy with it.

This was a state of things that could not last long, and he who had been so liberal with his spades' full of earth was speedily disarmed, and yet he was a popular favorite, and had done the thing so good-humouredly, that nobody touched him. Six or eight others who had brought spades and pickaxes now pushed forward to the work, and in an incredibly short space of time the grave of Miles, the butcher, seemed to be very nearly excavated.

Work of any kind is speedily executed when done with a wish to get through it, and never, perhaps, within the memory of man, was a grave opened in that churchyard with such a wonderful promptness. The excitement of the crowd grew intense – every available spot from which a view of the grave could be had, was occupied, for the last few minutes scarcely a remark had been uttered, and when at last the spade of one of the diggers struck upon something that sounded like wood, you might have heard a pin drop, and each one drew his breath more shortly than before.

"There he is," said the man, whose spade struck upon the coffin.

Those few words broke the spell, and there was a general murmur, while every individual present seemed to shift his position in his anxiety to obtain a better view of what was about to ensue.

The coffin having been found, there seemed to be an increased impetus given to the work; the earth was thrown out with a rapidity that seemed almost the quick result of the working of some machine, and those closest to the grave's brink crouched down and, intent as they were upon the progress of events, paid not the least attention to the damp earth that fell upon them, nor the frail brittle and humid remains of humanity that occasionally rolled to their feet. It was a scene of intense excitement.

And now the last few shovelfuls of earth that hid the top of the coffin were cast from the grave, and that narrow box which contained the mortal remains of the man, who was so well known while in life, was brought to the gaze of eyes which never had seemed likely to have looked upon him again.

The cry was now for ropes with which to raise the awkward mass, but these were not to be had; no one thought of providing himself with such appliances, so that the coffin could be raised to the brink only by massed strength.

The difficulty of doing this was immense, for there was nothing tangible to stand upon, and even when the mold from the sides was sufficiently cleared away that the handles of the coffin could be laid hold of, they came away immediately in the grasp of those who did so.

But the more trouble that presented itself to the accomplishment of the designs of the mob, the more intent that body seemed upon carrying out to the full extent their original designs.

Finding it quite impossible by bodily strength to raise the coffin of the butcher from the bottom of the hole, a boy was hastily dispatched to the village for ropes, and never did boy run with such speed before, for all his own curiosity was excited in the issue of an adventure that to his young imagination was appallingly interesting.

The boy came back with the necessary ropes almost immediately, and strong ropes were promptly slid under the inert mass, and twenty hands at once turned to the task of raising that receptacle of the dead from what had been presumed to be its last resting-place. The ropes strained and creaked, and many thought that they would burst asunder sooner than raise the coffin of the defunct butcher.

It is singular what reasons people find for backing their opinion.

"You may depend he's a vampyre," said one, "or it wouldn't be so difficult to get him out of the grave."

"Oh, there can be no mistake about that," said another one; "when did a natural Christian's coffin stick in the mud in that way?"

"Ah, to be sure," agreed another; "I knew no good would come of his goings on; he never was a decent sort of man like his neighbors, and many queer things have been said of him that I have no doubt are true enough, if we did but know the rights of them."

"Ah, but," said a young lad, thrusting his head between the two who were talking, "if he is a vampyre, how does he get out of his coffin at night with all that weight of earth on top of him?"

One of the men considered for a moment, and then finding no rational answer, he gave the boy a box on the ear, saying, "I should like to know what business that is of yours? Boys now-a-days ain't like the boys in my time; they think nothing now of putting their spoke in grown-up people's wheels, just as if their opinions were of any consequence."

Now by a vigorous effort, those who were tugging at the ropes succeeded in moving the coffin a little, and after that, it was loosened from that adhesive soil in which it lay, and it came up with considerable ease.

There was a shout of satisfaction at this result, while some of the congregation turned pale and trembled at the prospect of the sight which was about to present itself; the coffin was dragged from the grave's brink onto the long grass that flourished in the churchyard, and then they all looked at it for a time, and the men who had been most earnest in raising it wiped the perspiration from their brows, and seemed to shrink from the task of opening that receptacle of the dead now that it was in their power so to do.

Each man looked anxiously in his neighbors' face, and several audibly wondered why somebody else didn't open the coffin.

"There's no harm in it," said one; "if he's a vampyre, we ought to know it and, if he ain't, we can't do any hurt to a dead man."

"Oughtn't we to have the service for the dead?" asked one.

"Yes," said the impertinent boy who had before received the knock on the head, "I think we ought to have that read, back-wards."

This ingenious idea was paid back with a great many kicks and cuffs, which ought to have been sufficient to have warned him of the great danger of smarting off to his elders.

"Where's the use of shirking the job?" cried the man who had been so active in shoveling the mud upon the multitude; "why, you cowardly sneaking set of humbugs, you're half afraid, now."

"Afraid – afraid!" cried everybody; "who's afraid?"

"Ah, who's afraid?" said a little man, advancing, and assuming a heroic attitude; "I always notice if anybody's afraid, it's some big fellow with more bones than brains."

At this moment, the man to whom this reproach was more particularly leveled raised a horrible shout of terror, and cried out in frantic accents, "He's a-coming – he's a-coming!"

The little man fell at once into the grave, while the mob, with one accord, turned tail and fled in all directions, leaving him alone with the coffin. Such a fighting and kicking and scrambling ensued to get over the wall of the grave-yard that this great fellow, who had caused all the mischief, burst into peals of laughter, and the majority of the people became aware that it was a joke and came creeping back, looking as sheepish as possible.

Some got up very faint sorts of laughs, and said, "Very good," and swore they saw what big Dick meant from the first, and only ran to make the others run.

"Very good," said Dick. "I'm glad you enjoyed it, that's all. My eye, what a scampering there was among you. Where's my little friend, who was so infernally cunning about bones and brains?"

With some difficulty, the little man was extricated from the grave, and then, oh, for the consistency of a mob! They all laughed at him; those very people who, heedless of all the amenities of existence, had been trampling upon each other and roaring with terror, actually had the impudence to laugh at him, and call him a cowardly little rascal and say it served him right.

But such is popularity!

"Well, if nobody else won't open the coffin," said big Dick, "I will, so here goes. I knew the old fellow when he was alive and many a time he's damned me, and I damned him, so I ain't a-going to be afraid of him now he's dead. We was very intimate you see, 'cos we was the two heaviest men in the parish; there's a reason for everything."

"Ah, Dick's the fellow to do it," cried a number of persons; "there's nobody like Dick for opening a coffin; he's the man as don't care for nothing."

"Ah, you sniveling curs," cursed Dick, "I hate you. If it wasn't for my own satisfaction, I'd see you all jolly well…"

"Damned first," said the boy; "open the lid, Dick, let's have a look."

"Ah, you're a rum un," said Dick; "one after my own heart. I sometimes thinks as you must be a nephew, or some sort of relation of mine. How-so-ever, here goes. Who'd have thought that I should ever have had a look at old fat and thunder again? That's what I used to call him, and then he used to request me to go to hell, where I needn't turn round to light my blessed pipe."

"Hell – we know," said the boy; "why don't you open the lid, Dick?"

"I'm a going to," said Dick. And with that he placed the corner of a shovel between the lid and the coffin, and giving it a sudden wrench, he loosened it all down one side.

A shudder pervaded the multitude and, popularly speaking, you might have heard a pin drop in that crowded churchyard at that eventful moment.

Dick then proceeded to the other side, and executed the same maneuver.

"Now for it," he said; "we shall see him in a moment, and we'll think; we see him still."

"What a lark!" crowed the boy.

"You hold yer jaw, will yer? Who axed you for a remark, blow yer? What do you mean by squatting down there, like a cock-sparrow with a pain in his tail, hanging yer head, too, right over the coffin? Get out of the way of the cold meat, will yer!"

"A what, do you say, Dick?"

Dick threw down the spade, and laying hold of the coffin-lid with both hands, he lifted it off, and flung it on one side.

There was a visible movement and an exclamation among the multitude. Some were pushed down in the eager desire of those behind to obtain a sight of the ghastly remains of the butcher; those at a distance were frantic to get a glimpse, and the excitement was momentarily increasing.

They might all have spared themselves the trouble, for the coffin was empty. There was no dead butcher, nor any evidence of one ever having been there, not even the grave-clothes; the only thing in all in the receptacle of the dead was a brick. Dick's astonishment was so intense that his eyes and mouth kept opening together to such an extent, that it seemed doubtful when they would reach their extreme point of elongation. He then took up the brick and looked at it curiously, and turned it over and over, examined the ends and the sides with a critical eye, and at length he said, "Well, I'm blowed, here's a shift; he's changed himself into a blessed brick – my eye, here's a curiosity."

"But you don't mean to say that's the butcher?" asked the boy.

Dick reached over, and gave him a tap on the head with the brick. "There!" he said, "that's what I calls a ocular demonstration. Do you believe it now, you blessed infidel? What's more natural? He was an out-and-out brick while he was alive, and he's turned to a brick now he's dead."

"Give it to me, Dick," said the boy; "I should like to have that brick, just for the fun of the thing."

The Flight Of The Vampyre

"I sha'n't part with this here, it looks too blessed sensible; it's gaining on me every minute as a most remarkable likeness, damned if it ain't."

By this time the bewilderment of the mob had subsided; now that there was no dead butcher to look upon, they fancied themselves most grievously injured, and somehow or other, Dick, notwithstanding all his exertions in their service, was looked upon in the light of a showman who had promised some startling exhibition and then had disappointed his audience.

The first intimations he had of popular vengeance was a stone thrown at him, but Dick's eye happened to be on the fellow who threw it and, collaring him in a moment, he dealt him a cuff on the side of the head which confused his faculties for a week.

"Hark ye," he then cried with a loud voice, "don't interfere with me; it won't go down. There's something wrong here, and as one of yourselves, I'm as much interested in finding out what it is as any of you can possibly be. There seems to be some truth in this business; our old friend, the butcher, you see, is not in his grave; where is he then?"

The mob looked at each other, and none attempted to answer the question.

"Why, of course, he's the vampyre," said Dick, "and you may all of you expect to see him, in turn, come into your bed-room windows with a burst of speed, and lay hold of you like a million and a half of leeches rolled into one."

There was a general expression of horror, and then Dick continued, "You'd better all of you go home; I shall have no hand in pulling up any more of the coffins – this is a dose of salts for me. Of course you can do what you like."

"Pull them all up!" cried a voice; "pull them all up! Let's see how many vampyres there are in the churchyard."

"Well, it's no business of mine," said Dick; "but I wouldn't, if I was you."

"You may depend," said one, "that Dick knows something about it, or he wouldn't take it so easy."

"Ah! down with him," said the man who had received the box on the ears; "he's perhaps a vampyre himself."

The mob made a movement towards him, but Dick stood his ground and they paused again.

"Now, you're a cowardly set," he said; "because you're disappointed, you want to come upon me. Now I'll just show what a little thing will frighten you all again, and I warn beforehand it will, so you sha'n't say you didn't know it and were taken by surprise."

The mob looked at him, wondering what he was going to do. "Once! Twice! Thrice!" he said, and then he flung the brick up into the air an immense height, and shouted "heads," in a loud tone.

A general dispersion of the crowd ensued, and the brick fell in the centre of a very large circle indeed.

"There you are again," said Dick; "why, what a nice set you are!"

"What fun!" said the boy. "It's a famous coffin, this is," and he laid himself down in the butcher's last resting place. "I never was in a coffin before – it's snug enough."

"Ah, you are a rum 'un," said Dick; "you're such a inquiring genius, you is; you'll get your head in a hole one day, and not be able to get it out again, and then I shall see you a kicking. Hush! lay still – don't say anything."

"Good again," said the boy; "what shall I do?"

"Give a sort of a howl and a squeak, when they all come back again."

"Won't I!" said the boy, highly entertained at the idea; "I'll pop on the lid."

"There you we," said Dick; "damned if I don't adopt you, and bring you up to the science of nothing."

"Now, listen to me, good people all," added Dick; "I have really got something to say to you."

At this intimation, the people slowly gathered again round the grave. "Listen," said Dick, solemnly; "it strikes me there's some tremendous do going on."

"Yes, there is," said several who were foremost.

"It won't be long before you'll, all of you, be most damnably astonished, but let me beg of all you not to accuse me of having anything to do with it, provided I tell you all I know."

"No, Dick; we won't – we won't – we won't."

"Good then, listen. I don't know anything, but I'll tell you what I think, and that's as good. I don't think that this brick is the butcher, but I think, that when you least expect it – hush! come a little closer."

"Yes, yes; we are closer."

"Well, then, I say, when you least expect it, and when you ain't dreaming of such a thing, you'll hear something of my old friend as is dead and gone, that will astonish you all." Dick paused, and he gave the coffin a slight kick as intimation to the boy that he might as well be doing his part in the drama, upon which that ingenious young gentleman set up such a howl that even Dick jumped, so unearthly did if sound within the confines of that receptacle of the dead.

But if the effect upon him was great, what must it have been upon those whom it took completely unaware? For a moment or two they seemed completely paralyzed, and then they frightened the boy, for the shout of terror that rose from so many throats at once was positively alarming.

This jest of Dick's was the finale of that excursion for, before three minutes had elapsed, the churchyard was clear of all human occupants save himself and the boy who had played his part so well in the coffin. "Get out," said Dick; "it's all right – we've done 'em at last, and now you may depend upon it, they won't be in a hurry to come here again. You keep your own counsel, or else somebody will serve you out for this. I don't think you're altogether averse to a bit of fun, and if you keep yourself quiet, you'll have the satisfaction of hearing what's said about this affair in every tavern in the village, and no mistake.

Chapter 46
The Preparations for Leaving Bannerworth Hall – And the Mysterious Conduct of the Admiral and Mr. Chillingworth

It seemed now that with the agreement of all parties, Bannerworth Hall was to be abandoned and, notwithstanding Henry was loath to leave the ancient abode of his family, he felt his qualms overwhelmed by the others who seemed to be of opinion that it would be a prudent course to adopt. Thus he felt that it would not befit him to oppose the measure.

He now made his consent depend wholly upon the full and free agreement of every member of the family. "If," he informed his listeners, "there be any among us who will say to me 'Continue to keep open the house in which we have passed so many happy hours, and let the ancient home of our race still afford a shelter to us,' I shall feel myself bound to do so, but if both my mother and my brother agree to a departure from it, and that its hearth shall be left cold and desolate, be it so. I will not stand in the way of any unanimous wish or arrangement."

"We may consider that, then, as settled," said the Admiral, "for I have spoken to your brother and he is of our opinion. Therefore, my boy, we may all be off as soon as we can conveniently get under way."

"But my mother, what has she said?"

"Oh, there I don't know. You must speak to her yourself. I never, if I can help it, interfere with the women folks."

"If she consents, then I am willing."

"Will you ask her?"

"I will not ask her to leave, because I know what answer she would at once give, but she shall hear the proposition, and I will leave her to decide upon it, unbiased in her judgment by any stated opinion of mine upon the matter."

"Good. That'll do, and the proper way to put it, too. There's no mistake about that, I can tell you."

Henry, although he went through the ceremony of consulting his mother, had no doubt before he did so that she was sufficiently aware of the feelings and wishes of Flora to be prepared to yield a ready assent to the proposition of leaving the Hall.

Moreover, Mr. Marchdale had from the first been an advocate of such a course of proceeding, and Henry knew very well how strong an influence he had over Mrs. Bannerworth's mind, in consequence of the respect in which she held him as an old and valued friend.

He was, therefore, prepared for what his mother said, which was, "My dear Henry, you know that the wishes of my children since they have grown up and been capable of coming to a judgment for themselves have always been as law to me. If you all agree to leave this place, we shall do so."

"But will you leave it freely, mother?"

"Most freely I go with you all; what is it that has made this house pleasant to me but the presence in it of those who are so dear to me? If you all leave it, you take with you the only charms it ever possessed; so leaving it becomes in itself as nothing. I am quite ready to accompany you all anywhere, so long we keep together."

"Then, mother, we may consider that as settled."

"As you please."

"It is scarcely as I please. I must confess that I would have clung with a kind of superstitious reverence to this family house, but it may not be so. Those who are more able to come to correct conclusions, in consequence of their feelings not being sufficiently interested to lead them astray, have decided otherwise and, therefore, I am content to leave."

"Do not grieve at it, Henry. A cloud of misfortune has hung over us all since the garden of this house became the scene of an event which we can only remember with terror and shuddering."

"Two generations of our family must live and die before the remembrance of that circumstance can be obliterated. But we will think of it no more."

There can no doubt that the dreadful circumstances to which both Mrs. Bannerworth and Henry alluded, was the suicide of the father of the family in the gardens.

The reader will doubtless, too, recollect that at his last moments this unhappy individual was said to have uttered some incoherent words about some hidden money, and that the rapid hand of death alone seemed to prevent him from being explicit upon that subject, and left it merely a matter of conjecture.

As years had rolled on this affair, even as a subject of speculation, had ceased to occupy the minds of any of the Bannerworth family, and several of their friends, among whom was Mr. Marchdale, were decidedly of the opinion that the apparently pointed and mysterious words uttered were only the disordered wanderings of an intellect already hovering on the confines of eternity.

Indeed, far from any money – of any amount – being a disturbance to the last moments of the dissolute man whose vices and extravagances had brought his family to such ruin, it was pretty generally believed that he had committed suicide simply from a conviction of the impossibility of raising any more supplies of cash to enable him to carry on the dissolute career which he had pursued for so long.

But to resume the tale…

Henry at once communicated to the Admiral what his mother had said, and then the whole question regarding the removal being settled in the affirmative, nothing remained to be done but to set about it as quickly as possible.

The Bannerworths lived sufficiently distant from the town to be out of earshot of the disturbances which were then taking place, and so completely isolated were they from all sort of society that they had no notion of the popular disturbance which Varney the vampyre had given rise to.

It was not until the following morning that Mr. Chillingworth, who had been home in the meantime, brought word of what had taken place, and that great commotion was still occurring in the town, and that the civil authorities finding themselves by far too weak to contend against the popular will, had sent for assistance to a garrison town some twenty miles distant.

It was a great grief to the Bannerworth family to hear these tidings, not that they were in any way, except as victims, accessory to creating the disturbance about the vampyre, but it seemed to promise a kind of notoriety which they might well shrink from, and which they were just the people to view with dislike.

View the matter how we like, it is not to be considered as at all probable that the Bannerworth family would remain long in ignorance of what a great sensation they had created unwittingly in the neighborhood.

The very reasons which had induced their servants to leave their establishment and prefer throwing themselves completely out of a workplace rather than remain in so ill-omened a house, were sure to be discussed far and wide.

And that, when they came to consider it, would suffice to form another good and substantial reason for leaving the Hall and seeking a refuge in obscurity from the extremely troublesome sort of popularity incidental to their peculiar situation.

Mr. Chillingworth felt uncommonly reluctant to tell them all that had taken place; although he was well aware that the proceedings of the riotous mob had not terminated with the little disappointment at the old ruin to which they had so effectually chased Varney, the vampyre, only to lose him so singularly when he got there.

No doubt he informed the Admiral about the uproar that was going on in the town, for the latter did hint a little of it to Henry Bannerworth. "Hilloa!" he said to Henry, as he saw him walking in the garden; "it strikes me that if you or your ship's crew continues in these latitudes, you'll get as notorious as the Flying Dutchman in the southern ocean."

"How do you mean?" Henry inquired in puzzled tones.

"Why, it's a sure going proverb to say that a nod's as good as a wink, but the fact is, it's getting rather too well known to be pleasant that a vampyre has struck up a rather close acquaintance with your family. I understand there's a precious row in the town."

"Indeed!"

"Yes; bother the particulars, for I don't know them, but, hark ye, by to-morrow I'll have found a place for you to go to, so pack up the sticks, get all your stores ready to clear out, and make yourself scarce from this place."

"I understand you," said Henry; "we have become the subject of popular rumor; I've only to beg of you, Admiral, that you'll say nothing of this to Flora; she has already suffered enough, Heaven knows; do not let her have the additional affliction of thinking that her name is made familiar in every pothouse in the town."

"Leave me alone for that," said the Admiral. "Do you think I'm an ass?"

"Ay, ay," said Jack Pringle, who came in at that moment, and thought the question was addressed to him.

"Who spoke to you, you bad-looking horse-marine[ix]?"

"Me, a horse-marine! Didn't you ask a plain question of a fellow, and get a plain answer?"

"Why, you son-of-a-bad-looking-gun, what do you mean by that? I tell you what it is, Jack; I've let you come sneaking too often on the quarter-deck, and now you come poking your fun at your officers, you rascal!"

"I, poking fun!" exclaimed Jack; "I couldn't think of such a thing. I should just as soon think of your making a joke as me."

"Now, I tell you what it is; I shall just strike you off the ship's books, and you shall just go and cruise by yourself; I've done with you."

"Go and tell that to the marines[x], if you like," said Jack. "I ain't done with you yet, for a jolly long watch. Why, what do you suppose would become of you, you great baby, without me? Ain't I always a conveying you from place to place, and steering you through all sorts of difficulties?"

"Damn your impudence!"

"Well then, damn yours."

"Shiver my timbers!"

"Ay, you may do what you like with your own timbers."

"And you won't leave me?"

"Startlingly, not."

"Come here, then?"

Jack might have expected a gratuity, for he advanced with alacrity.

"There," said the Admiral, as he laid his stick across his shoulders; "that's your last month's wages; don't spend it all at once."

"Well, I'm damned!" said Jack; "who'd have thought of that? He's turning rumgumptious, and no mistake. Howsomedever, I must turn it over in my mind, and be even with him, somehow. I owes him one for that. I say, Admiral."

"What now, you lubber?"[xi]

"Nothing; turn that over in your mind," and away Jack walked, not quite satisfied, but feeling that he had made a demonstration of attack.

As for the Admiral, he considered that the thump he had given Jack with the stick, and it was no gentle one, as a decided balancing of accounts up to that period, and as he remained likewise master of the field, he was upon the whole very well satisfied.

These last few words which had been spoken to Henry by Admiral Bell, more than any others, induced him to hasten his departure from Bannerworth Hall; he had walked away when the altercation between Jack Pringle and the Admiral began, for he had seen sufficient of those wordy conflicts between those originals to be quite satisfied that neither of them meant what he said of a discouraging character towards the other, and that far from there being any unfriendly feeling contingent upon those little affairs, they were only a species of friendly sparring, which both parties enjoyed extremely. Henry went directly to Flora, and he said to her, "Since we are all agreed upon the necessity, or at all events upon the expediency of a departure from the Hall, I think, sister, the sooner we carry out that determination the better and the pleasanter for us all it will be. Do you think you could remove so hastily as tomorrow?"

"Tomorrow! That is soon indeed."

"I grant you that it is so, but Admiral Bell assures me that he will have everything in readiness, and a place provided for us to go to by then."

"Would it be possible to depart from a house like this so very quickly?"

"Yes, sister. If you look around you, you will see that a great portion of the comforts you enjoy in this mansion belong to it as a part of its very structure, and are not removable; what we really have to take away is very little. The urgent lack of money during our father's lifetime induced him, as you may recollect, at various times to part with much that was ornamental, as well as useful, which was in the Hall. You will recollect that we seldom returned from those little continental tours without finding some old familiar objects gone, which, upon inquiry, we found had been turned into money to meet some more than usually pressing demand."

"That is true, brother; I recollect well."

"So that, upon the whole, sister, there is little to remove."

"Well, well, be it so. I will prepare our mother for this sudden step. Believe me, my heart goes with it. And it is certainly better, as you say, that the act should be quickly consummated, rather than left hanging in terror over our minds."

"Then I'll consider that as settled," Henry agreed much pleased.

Chapter 47
The Departure from the Hall – The Night Watch – The Alarm

Mrs. Bannerworth's consent having been already given to the departure from the Hall, she said at once, when appealed to, that she was quite ready to go at any time her children thought best.

Upon hearing this, Henry sought the Admiral and told him as much, at the same time adding, "My sister feared that we should have considerable trouble in the removal, but I have convinced her that such will not be the case, as we are by no means overburdened with cumbrous property."

"Cumbrous property," said the Admiral, "why, what do you mean? I beg leave to say that when I took the house, I took the table and chairs with it. Damn it, what good do you suppose an empty house is to me?"

"The tables and chairs?"

"Yes. I took the house just as it stands. Don't try and bamboozle me out of it. I tell you, you've nothing to move but yourselves and immediate personal effects."

"I was not aware, Admiral, that that was your plan."

"Well then, now you are aware, so listen to me. I've circumvented the enemy too often not to know how to get up a plot. Jack and I have managed it all. Tomorrow evening, after dark, but before the moon's got high enough to throw any light, you and your brother, and Miss Flora and your mother, will come out of the house, and Jack and I will lead you where you're to go to. There's plenty of furniture where you're a-going, and so you will get off free, without anybody knowing anything about it."

"Well, Admiral, I've said it before, and it is the unanimous opinion of us all, that everything should be left to you. You have proven yourself too good a friend to us for us to hesitate at all in obeying your commands. Arrange everything, I pray you, according to your wishes and feelings, and you will find there shall be no arguing on our parts."

"That's right; there's nothing like giving the command post to one person. There's no good done without. Now I'll manage it all. Mind you, seven o'clock tomorrow evening everything is to be ready and you will all be prepared to leave the Hall."

"It shall be so."

"Who's that giving such a thundering ring at the gate?"

"I don't know. We have few visitors and no servants, so I must even be my own gate porter."

Henry walked to the gate and opened it. A servant in a handsome livery stepped a pace or two into the garden.

"Well?" asked Henry.

"Is Mr. Henry Bannerworth within, or Admiral Bell?"

"Both," cried the Admiral. "I'm Admiral Bell, and this is Mr. Henry Bannerworth. What do you want with us, you damned gingerbread-looking flunkey?"

"Sir, my master sends his compliments – his very best compliments – and he wants to know how you are after your flurry."

"What?"

"After your – a – a – flurry and excitement."

"Who is your master?" asked Henry.

"Sir Francis Varney."

"The devil!" said the Admiral; "if that don't beat all the impudence I ever came near. Our flurry! Ah! I like that fellow. Just go and tell him…"

"No, no," said Henry, interposing, "send back no message. Say to your master, fellow, that Mr. Henry Bannerworth feels that not only has he no claim to Sir Francis Varney's courtesy, but that he should rather be without it."

"Oh, ha!" said the footman, adjusting his collar; "very good. This seems a damned, old-fashioned, outlandish place of yours. Any ale?"

"Now, shiver my hulks!" roared the Admiral.

"Hush! Hush!" said Henry; "who knows but there may be a design in this? We have no ale."

"Oh, ah! damne! – dry as dust, by God! What does the old Commodore say? Any message, my ancient Greek?"

"No, thank you," blustered the Admiral; "bless you, nothing. What did you give for that waistcoat, damn you? Ha! Ha! You're a clever fellow."

"Ah! The old gentleman's ill. However, I'll take back his compliments, and that he's much obliged at Sir Francis's condescension. At the same time, I suppose I may place in my eye what I may get out of either of you, without hindering me seeing my way back. Ha! Ha! Adieu – adieu."

The Admiral's calmness during the latter part of the dialogue arose from the fact that, over the flunkey's shoulder and at some little distance off, he saw Jack Pringle taking off his jacket and rolling up his sleeves in that deliberate sort of way that seemed to imply a determination of setting about some species of work that combined the pleasant with the useful.

Jack executed many nods to and winks at the livery-servant, and jerked his thumb likewise in the direction of a pump near at hand.

And now the conference was ended and Sir Francis's messenger turned to go, but Jack Pringle bothered him completely, for he danced round him in such a singular manner, that, turn which way he would, there stood Jack Pringle, in some grotesque attitude, intercepting him, and so he edged him on, till he got him to the pump.

"Jack," said the Admiral.

"Ay, ay, sir."

"Don't pump on that fellow now."

"Ay, ay, sir;" he said giving the Admiral a broad wink, "give us a hand."

Jack laid hold of Varney's servant by both his ears, and holding him under the pump, kicked his shins until he completely gathered him beneath the spout. It was in vain that he shouted, "Murder! Help! Fire! Thieves!" Jack was inexorable; the Admiral took hold of the pump handle and began to pump energetically.

Jack turned the fellow's head about in a very scientific manner, so as to give him a fair dose of hydropathic treatment, and in a few minutes, a human was never more thoroughly saturated with moisture than was Sir Francis Varney's servant. He had left off hallooing for aid, for he found that whenever he did so, Jack held his mouth under the spout, which was decidedly unpleasant; so, with a patience that looked like heroic fortitude, he was compelled to wait until the Admiral was tired of pumping.

"Very good," the Admiral declared at length. "Now, Jack, for fear this fellow catches cold, be so good as to get a horsewhip, and see him off the premises with it."

"Ay, ay, sir," said Jack. "And I say, old fellow," he told his victim, "you can take back all our blessed compliments now, and say you've been flurried a little yourself, and if so be as you came here as dry as dust, damne, you go back as wet as a mop. Won't it do to kick him out, sir?"

"Very well – as you please, Jack."

"Then here goes," and Jack proceeded to kick the shivering man from the garden with a vehemence that soon convinced him of the necessity of getting out of it as quickly as possible.

How it was that Sir Francis Varney, after that fearful race he had had, got home again across the fields free from all danger and back to his own house, from whence he sent so cool and insolent a message, they could not conceive.

But such must certainly be the fact; somehow or another he had escaped all danger, and with a calm insolence peculiar to the man, he had no doubt adopted the present mode of signifying as much to the Bannerworths.

The insolence of his servant was, no doubt, a matter of pre-arrangement with that individual; however, he might have set about it *con amore*. As for the termination of the adventure, that had not been at all calculated upon, but like most tools of other people's insolence or ambition, the insolence of the underling had received both his own punishment and his master's.

Gentle reader, we will now leave the Bannerworths to their packing, and return to the village and the mystery of the missing butcher's body.

*****

Was the mob satisfied with what had occurred in the churchyard? They were not, and that night was to witness the perpetration of a melancholy outrage, such as the history of the time presents no parallel to.

The Flight Of The Vampyre

The finding of a brick in the coffin of the butcher instead of the body of that individual, soon spread as a piece of startling intelligence all over the place, and the obvious deduction that was drawn from the circumstance seemed to be that the deceased butcher was unquestionably a vampyre, and out upon some expedition at the very time when his coffin was searched.

How he had originally gotten out of that receptacle for the dead was certainly a mystery, but the story was none the worse for that lack of information. Indeed, an ingenious individual found a solution for that part of the business, for, as he said, nothing was more natural, when anybody died who was capable of becoming a vampyre, than for other vampyres who knew it to dig him up, and lay him out in the cold beams of the moonlight until he acquired the same sort of vitality they themselves possessed and joined their horrible fraternity.

In lieu of a better explanation – and after all, it was no bad one – this theory was generally well received, and with a shuddering horror people asked themselves, if the whole of the churchyard were excavated, just how many coffins would be found tenantless by the dead which had been supposed, by simpleminded people, to inhabit them.

The arrival of a body of Dragoons[xii] that evening prevented any renewed attack upon the sacred precincts of the churchyard, and it was a strange and startling thing to see that country town under military surveillance, and sentinels posted at its principal buildings.

This measure smothered the vengeance of the crowd, and insured for a time the safety of Sir Francis Varney, for no considerable body of persons could assemble for the purpose of attacking his house again without being followed; so such a step was not attempted.

It had so happened, however, that on that very day, the funeral of a young man was to have taken place; he had stayed for a time at that same inn where Admiral Bell was first introduced to the reader. He had become seriously ill, and after a few days of indisposition which had puzzled the country practitioners, breathed his last.

He was to have been buried in the village churchyard on the very day of the riot and confusion incidental to the exhumation of the coffin of the butcher; probably from that circumstance we may deduce the presence of the clergyman in canonicals at the period of the riot.

When it was found that so disorderly a mob possessed the churchyard, the idea of burying the stranger that day was abandoned, but still all would have gone on quietly as regarded him, had it not been for the folly of one of the chamber-maids at the tavern.

This woman, with all the love of gossip incidental to her class, had from the first entered so fully into all the particulars concerning vampyres that she fairly might be considered to be a little deranged on that head. Her imagination had been so worked upon that she was in an unfit state to think of anything else, and if ever upon anybody a stern and revolting superstition was calculated to produce dreadful effects, it was upon this woman.

The town was tolerably quiet; the presence of the soldiery had frightened some and amused others, and no doubt the night would have passed off serenely, had she not suddenly rushed into the streets, and with bewildered accents and frantic gestures she shouted, "A vampyre – a vampyre – a vampyre!"

These words soon collected a crowd around her, and then, with screaming accents, which would have been quite enough to convince any reflecting person that she had actually gone distracted upon that point, she cried, "Come into the house – come into the house – come into the house! Look upon the dead body that should have been in its grave; it's fresher now than on the day on which it died, and there's color in its cheeks. A vampyre – a vampyre – a vampyre! Heaven save us from a vampyre!"

The strange, infuriated, maniacal manner in which these words were uttered produced an astonishingly exciting effect among the mob. Several women screamed, and some few fainted. The torch was laid again to the altar of popular feeling, and the fierce flame of superstition burnt brightly and fiercely.

Some twenty or thirty persons, with shouts and exclamations, rushed into the inn, while the woman who had created the disturbance still continued to rave, tearing her hair, and shrieking at intervals, until she fell exhausted upon the pavement.

Soon from a hundred throats rose that dreadful cry of "A vampyre – a vampyre!" The alarm was given throughout the whole town; the bugles of the military sounded; there was a clash of arms – the shrieks of women; although the premonitory symptoms of such a riot as was not likely to be quelled without bloodshed and considerable disaster.

It is truly astonishing the effect which one weak or vicious-minded person can produce upon a multitude. Here was a woman whose opinion would have been accounted valueless upon the most common-place subject, and whose word would not have passed for two cents, setting a whole town by the ears by force of nothing but her sheer brutal ignorance.

It is a notorious physiological fact that, after four or five days, or even a week, the bodies of many persons assume an appearance of freshness, such as might have been looked for in vain immediately after death.

It is one of the most insidious processes of that decay which appears to regret using its "offensive fingers to mar the lines where beauty lingers." But what did the chamber-maid know of physiology? Probably, she would have asked if it was anything good to eat, and so, of course, having her head full of vampyres, she must produce so lamentable a scene of confusion, the results of which we almost sicken at detailing.

Chapter 48
The Stake and the Dead Body

The mob seemed from the first to have an impression that, as regarded the military force, no very serious results would arise from that quarter, for it was not to be supposed that on an occasion which could not possibly arouse any ill blood on the part of the soldiery, or on which they could have the least personal feeling, they would like to get a bad name, which would stick to them for years to come.

It was not a political riot on which men might be supposed in consequence of differing in opinion to have their passions inflamed. Thus, although the call of the civil authorities for military aid had been acceded to, yet it was hoped and, indeed almost understood by the officers, that their operations would be confined more to a demonstration of power than anything else.

Besides, some of the men had got talking to the townspeople and had heard all about the vampyre story, and not being of the most refined or educated class themselves, they felt rather interested than otherwise in the affair.

Under these circumstances then, we are inclined to think that the disorderly mob of that inn did not have such a wholesome fear as it was most certainly intended they should have of the red coats. Then again, they were not attacking the churchyard which in the first case was the main point in dispute, and about which the authorities had felt so very sore, inasmuch as they felt that if once the common people found out that the sanctity of such places could be outraged which impunity, they would lose their reverence for the church; that is to say in truth, for the host of persons who live well and get fat in this country by the trade of religion.

Consequently, this churchyard was the main point of defense, and it was zealously looked to when it did not need it, while the public-house where there really was mischief half unguarded.

There are always in all communities, whether large or small, a number of persons who really have, or fancy they have, something to gain by disturbance. These people, of course, care not for what pretext with which the public peace is violated; so long as there is a row, and with something like an excuse for running into other peoples' houses, they are satisfied.

To get into a public-house under such circumstances is an unexpected treat, and thus when the mob rushed into the inn with many symptoms of fury and excitement, there went with the leaders of the disturbance a number of persons who never thought of getting further than the bar, where they attacked the keg-taps with an enthusiasm which showed how great was their love for ardent compounds.

Leaving these persons behind, we will follow those who with a real superstition, and a furious interest in the affair of the vampyre, made their way towards the upper chamber, determined to see for themselves if there were truth in the statement so alarmingly made by the woman who had created such an emotion.

It is astonishing what people will do in crowds, in comparison with the acts that they would be able to commit individually. There is usually a calmness, a sanctity, a sublimity about death, which irresistibly induces a respect for its presence from the educated as well as the illiterate, and let the object of the fell-destroyer's presence be whom it may, the very consciousness that death has claimed it for its own, invests it with a halo of respect to which in life the individual could never aspire.

Let us precede these furious rioters for a few moments and look upon the chamber of the dead – that chamber, which for a whole week had been looked upon with a kind of shuddering terror – that chamber which had been darkened by having its sources of light closed as if it were a kind of disrespect to the dead to allow the pleasant sunshine to fall upon the faded form.

And every inhabitant of that house, upon ascending and descending its intricate and ancient staircases, had walked with a quiet and subdued step past that one particular door.

Even the tones of voice in which they spoke to each other, while they knew that that sad remnant of mortality was in the house, was quiet and subdued, as if the repose of death was but a mortal sleep and could be broken by rude sounds.

Ay, even some of these very persons who now with loud and boisterous clamor had rushed into the place had visited the house and talked in whispers, but then they were alone, and men will do in throngs acts which, individually, they would shrink from with compunction or cowardice, call it which we will.

The chamber of death is upon the second story of the house. It is a back room, with windows commanding a view of that half garden, half farm-yard, which we find generally belonging to country inns.

But now the shutters were closed with the exception of one small opening that in daylight would have admitted a straggling ray of light to fall upon the corpse. Now, however, that the somber shades of evening had wrapped everything in gloom, the room appeared in total darkness, so that the most of those adventurers who had ventured into the place shrunk back until lights were procured from the lower part of the house.

A dim oil lamp in a niche sufficiently lighted the staircase, and by the friendly aid of its glimmering beams, they had found their way up to the landing tolerably easily, not thinking about the necessity of having lights with which to enter the apartments until they found them in utter darkness.

These requisites were speedily procured from the kitchen of the inn. Indeed, anything that was wanted was laid hold of without the least word or remark to the people of the place, as if might, from that evening forward, was understood to constitute right in that town.

Up to this point no one had taken a very prominent part in the attack upon the inn, if attack it could be called, but now the man whom chance or his own nimbleness made the first of the throng, assumed to himself a sort of control over his companions, and turning to them, he said, "Hark ye, my friends; we'll do everything quietly and properly; so I think we'd better, three or four, of us go in at once, arm-in-arm."

"Psha!" cried one who had just arrived with a light; "it's your cowardice that speaks. I'll go in first; let those follow me who like, and those who are afraid may remain where they are."

He at once dashed into the room, and this immediately broke the spell of fear which was beginning to creep over the others in consequence of the timid suggestion of the man who, up to that moment, had been first and foremost in the enterprise.

In an instant the chamber was half filled with persons, four or five of whom carried lights; so that as it was not very big, it was sufficiently illuminated for every object in it to be clearly visible.

There was the bed, smooth and unruffled, as if waiting for some expected guest; while close by its side a coffin, supported upon trestles, over which a sheet was partially thrown, contained the sad remains of him who little expected in life that, after death, he should be stigmatized as a example of one of the ghastliest superstitions that ever found a home in the human imagination.

It was evident that someone had been in the room, and there could be no doubt that this visitor had been the woman whose excited fancy had led her to look upon the face of the corpse, for the sheet was drawn aside just sufficiently to reveal the countenance.

The fact was that the stranger was unknown at the inn, or probably before this the coffin lid would have been screwed on, but it was hoped up to the last moment, as advertisements had been put into the county papers, that someone would come forward to identify and claim him. Such, however, had not been the case, and so it had been determined to go ahead and bury him.

The presence of so many persons at once prevented any individual from exhibiting, even if he felt it, any superstitious fears about approaching the coffin, and so with one accord they surrounded it and looked upon the face of the dead.

There was nothing repulsive in the countenance that they gazed upon. The fact was that decomposition had sufficiently advanced to induce a relaxation of the muscles, so that an appearance of calmness and repose had crept over the face which it did not wear immediately after death.

It happened, too, that the face was full of flesh, for the death had been sudden, and there had not been that wasting away of the muscle which makes the skin cling, as it were, to the bone, when the ravages of long disease have exhausted the physical frame.

There was unquestionably a plumpness, a freshness, and a sort of vitality about the countenance that was remarkable.

For a few moments there was a deathlike stillness in the apartment, and then one voice broke the silence by exclaiming, "He's a vampyre, and he has come here to die. Well he knows he'd be taken up by Sir Francis Varney, and revivified to become one of the crew."

"Yes, yes," cried several voices at once; "a vampyre! a vampyre!"

"Hold a moment," cried one; "let us find somebody in the house who has seen him some days ago, and then we can ascertain if there's any difference in his looks."

This suggestion was agreed to, and a couple of stout men ran down stairs; they returned in a few moments with a trembling waiter, whom they had caught in the passage and forced to accompany them to the room.

This man seemed to think that he was to be made a dreadful example of some sort of way and, as he was dragged into the room, he trembled and looked as pale as death.

"What have I done, gentlemen?" he said; "I ain't a vampyre. Don't be driving a stake through me. I assure you gentlemen, I'm only a waiter, and have been for a matter of five-and-twenty years."

"You'll be done no harm to," said one of his captors; "you've only got to answer a question that will be put to you."

"Oh, well, certainly, gentlemen; anything you please."

"Look upon the face of that corpse."

"Certainly, certainly – directly."

"Have you ever seen it before?"

"Seen it before! Lord bless you! Yes, a dozen of times. I seed him afore he died, and I seed him after, and when the undertaker's men came, I came up with them and I seed 'em up put him in his coffin. You see I kept an eye on them gentlemen, 'cos I knows well enough what they is. A cousin of mine was in the trade, and he assures me as one of 'em always brings a tooth-drawing concern in his pocket, and looks in the mouth of the blessed corpse to see if there's a blessed tooth worth pulling out."

"Hold your tongue," said one; "we want none of your nonsense. Do you see any difference now in the face of the corpse to what it was some days since?"

The Flight Of The Vampyre

"Well, I don't know; somehow, it don't look so rum"

"Does it look fresher?"

"Well, somehow or another, now you mention it, it's very odd, but it does.

"Enough," cried the man who had questioned him, with considerable excitement of manner. Neighbors are we to have our wives and our children scared to death by vampyres?"

"No – no!" cried everybody.

"Is not this, then, one of that dreadful order of beings?"

"Yes – yes; what's to be done?"

"Drive a stake through the body, and so prevent the possibility of anything in the shape of a restoration."

This was a terrible proposition, and even those who felt most strongly upon the subject, and had their fears most awakened, shrank from carrying it into effect. Others applauded it, although they determined in their own minds to keep far enough off from the execution of the job, which they hoped would devolve upon others, so that they might have all the security of feeling that such a process had been gone through with the supposed vampyre, without being in any way committed by the dreadful act.

Nothing was easier than to procure a stake from the garden in the rear of the premises, but it was one thing to have the means at hand of carrying into effect so dreadful a proposition, and another to actually do it.

For the credit of human nature, we regret that even then, when civilization and popular education had by no means made such rapid strides as they have in our times, such a proposition should be entertained for a moment, but so it was, and just as an alarm was given that a party of the soldiery had reached the inn, and had taken possession of the doorway with a determination to arrest the rioters, a strong hedge-stake had been procured, and everything was in readiness for the perpetration of the horrible deed.

Even then those in the room, for they were tolerably sober, would probably have revolted from the execution of so fearful an act, but the entrance of a party of military into the lower portion of the tavern induced those who had been making free with the strong liquors below to make a rush upstairs to their companions with the hope of escaping detection of the petty larceny if they got into trouble on account of the riot.

These persons, infuriated by drink, were capable of anything, and to them; accordingly, the more sober parties gladly surrendered the disagreeable job of rendering the supposed vampyre truly dead by driving a hedge-stake through his body — a proceeding which, it was currently believed, inflicted so much physical injury to the frame as to render his resuscitation out of the question.

The cries of alarm from below, joined now to the shouts of those mad rioters, produced a scene of dreadful confusion.

We cannot, for we revolt at the need to do so, describe the dreadful outrage which was committed upon the corpse; suffice it that two or three rioters, maddened by drink and incited by others, plunged the hedge-stake through the body, and there left it as a sickening and a horrible spectacle to anyone who might cast his eyes upon it.

With such violence had the frightful and inhuman deed been committed that the bottom of the coffin was perforated by the stake, so that the corpse was actually nailed to its last earthly tenement.

Some asserted that at that moment an audible groan came from the dead man, and that this arose from the extinguishment of that remnant of life which remained in him on account of his being a vampyre who would have been brought into full existence if the body had been placed in the rays of the moon, according to the popular superstition upon that subject.

Others were quite ready to swear that at the moment the stake was used, there was a visible convulsion of all the limbs, and that the countenance before so placid and so calm became immediately distorted as if with agony.

But we have done with these horrible surmises; the dreadful deed has been committed, and wild, ungovernable superstition has had, for a time, its sway over the ignorant and debased.

Chapter 49
The Mob's Capture

The soldiery had been sent for from their principal station near the churchyard, and they had advanced with some degree of reluctance to quell what they considered as nothing other than a drunken brawl at a public-house, which they really considered they ought not to be called to interfere with.

When, however, the party reached the spot and heard what a confusion there was, and saw in what numbers the rioters were assembling, it became evident to them that the case was of a more serious complexion than they had at first imagined and, consequently they felt that their professional dignity was not so much compromised by their interference with the lawless proceedings.

Some of the constabulary of the town were there, and to them the soldiers promised they would hand whatever prisoners they took.

This was all that the civil authorities of the town required, and they hoped that after making prisoners of a few of the ringleaders of the riotous proceedings, the rest would disperse, preventing the necessity of capturing them.

Be it known, however, that both military and civil authorities were completely ignorant of the dreadful outrage against all common decency which had been committed within the public-house.

The door was well guarded, and the question now was how the rioters were to be made to come downstairs and be captured, and this was likely to remain a question so long as no means were adopted to make them descend. After a time, it was agreed that a couple of troopers would march upstairs with a constable to allow him to secure anyone who seemed a principal in the riot.

But this only had the effect of driving those who were on the second-floor and saw the approach of the two soldiers whom they thought were backed by the whole of their comrades, up a narrow staircase to a third-floor consisting of lofts instead of actual rooms, but still, for the time it was a refuge, and owning to the extreme narrowness of the approach to it, which consisted of nearly a perpendicular staircase, with any degree of tact or method it might have been admirably defended.

The Flight Of The Vampyre

In the hurry and scramble all the lights were left behind, and when the two soldiers and constables entered the room where the corpse had lain, they became for the first time aware of what a horrible purpose had been carried out by the infuriated mob.

The sight was one of perfect horror, and hardened to scenes which might strike other people as being terrible as these soldiers might be supposed to be by their very profession, they were actually sickened at the sight which the mutilated corpse presented, and turned aside with horror.

These feelings soon gave way to anger and animosity against the crowd who could be guilty of such an atrocious outrage, and for the first time a strong and interested vengeance against the mob pervaded the breasts of those who were brought to act against it.

One of the soldiers ran downstairs to the door and reported the scene which was to be seen above. A determination was instantly come to, to capture as many as possible of those who had been concerned in so diabolical an outrage, and leaving a guard of five men at the door the remainder of the party ascended the staircase, determined upon storming the last refuge of the rioters and dragging them to justice.

The report of these proceedings that were taking place at the inn spread quickly over the whole town, and soon a large a mob of the disorderly and the idle was assembled outside the inn.

This mob appeared for a time to only watch the proceedings. It seemed a rather hazardous thing to interfere with the soldiers, whose carbines looked like formidable and troublesome weapons.

With true mob courage they left the minority of their comrades, who were within the house, to their fate, and after a whispered conference from one to the other, they suddenly turned in a body and began to make for the outskirts of the town.

They then separated as if by common consent. They straggled out into the open country by twos and threes, consolidating again into a mass when they had got some distance off, and were clear of any exertions that could be made by the soldiery to stop them.

The cry then rose of "Down with Sir Francis Varney — slay him — burn his house — death to all vampyres!" and at a rapid pace they proceeded in the direction of his mansion.

We will leave this mob, however, for the present, and turn our attention to those who are at the inn and are certainly in a position of some jeopardy. Their numbers were not great, and they were unarmed;

certainly, their best chance would have been to have surrendered, but that was a measure which, if the sober ones had felt inclined to take, those who were infuriated and half maddened with drink would not have agreed to on any account.

A furious resistance was to be expected from these maddened individuals, and what means the soldiery was likely to use for the purpose of storming this last retreat was a matter of rather anxious conjecture.

In the case of a regular enemy there would not have been much difficulty, but here the capture of certain persons, not their destruction, was the object, and how that was to be accomplished by fair means was a question which nobody felt very competent to solve.

Determination will do wonders, and although the rioters numbered over forty, notwithstanding all the desertions from their rank, and only seventeen or eighteen soldiers marched into the inn; we shall perceive that the soldiers succeeded in accomplishing their object without any maneuvering at all.

The space in which the rioters were confined was low, narrow, and inconvenient, as well as dark.

They found very few weapons of defense, and yet there were some which, to do them but common credit, they used as effectually as possible.

These attics, or lofts, were used as lumber-rooms[xiii], and had been so for years, so that there was a collection of old boxes, broken pieces of furniture, and other matters, which will, in defiance of everything and everybody, collect in a house.

These were a formidable means of defense, if not of offence, down a very narrow staircase, had they been used with judgment.

Some of the rioters, who were drunk enough to be fool-hardy, collected a few of these articles at the top of the staircase, and swore they would smash anybody who should attempt to come up to them, a threat easier uttered than executed.

And besides, after all, if their position had been impregnable they must come down eventually, or be starved out.

But the soldiers were not at liberty to adopt so slow a process of overcoming their enemy, and up the second-floor staircase they went, with a determination of making short work of the business.

They paused a moment, by word of command, on the landing, and then after this slight pause, the word was given to advance.

"Fire," said the officer who was in charge, and it appeared that he had made some arrangements as to how the order was to be obeyed, for the first man fired his carbine then fell to his knees, enabling the second man to fire his carbine and then scramble over his prostrate comrade; after which he stooped, and the third fired his carbine likewise, and then hurried forward in the same manner.

At the first sound of the firearms the rioters were taken completely by surprise; they had not had the least notion of affairs getting to such a length. The smell of the powder, the loud report, and the sensation of positive danger that accompanied these phenomena, alarmed them most terrifically; so that, in point of fact, with the exception of the empty chest that was thrown down in the way of the first soldier attempting to climb the stairs, no further idea of defense seemed in any way to find a place in the hearts of the besieged.

The rioters scrambled one over the other in their eagerness to get as far as possible from immediate danger, which of course they conceived existed in the most imminent degree the nearer to the door they were.

Such was the state of terror into which they were thrown that each one at the moment believed himself shot, and the soldiers had overcome all the real difficulties in getting possession of what might thus be called the citadel of the inn, before those men who had been so valorous a short time since recovered from the tremendous fright into which they had been thrown.

We need hardly say that the carbines were loaded with blank cartridges, for there was neither a disposition nor a necessity for taking the lives of these misguided people.

It was the suddenness and the steadiness of the attack that had done all the mischief to their cause, but now, before they recovered from the surprise of having their position so completely taken by storm, they were handed down stairs, one by one, from soldier to soldier, and into the custody of the civil authorities.

In order to secure the safe keeping of so large a body of prisoners, the constables, who were in a great minority, placed handcuffs upon some of the most capable of resistance; so what with those who were thus secured, and those who were terrified into submission, there was not a man of all the lot who had taken refuge in the attics of the public-house but was a prisoner.

At the sound of fire-arms, the women who were outside the inn had, of course, raised a prodigious clamor.

They believed that every bullet must have done some serious mischief to the townspeople, and it was only after one of the soldiers, a non-commissioned officer, assured them of the innocuous nature of the proceeding that any degree of equanimity was restored.

"Silence!" he cried; "what are you howling about? Do you fancy that we've nothing better to do than to shoot a parcel of fellows that are not worth the bullets that would be lodged in their confounded carcasses?"

"But we heard guns," a woman cried loudly.

"Of course you did; it's the powder that makes the noise, not the bullet. You'll see them all brought out safe wind and limb."

This assurance satisfied the women to a certain extent, and such had been their fear that they should have had to look upon the spectacle of death, or of grievous wounds, that they were comparatively satisfied when they saw husbands, fathers, and brothers in the custody of the town officers.

And very sheepish some of the fellows looked when they were handed down and handcuffed; especially when they learned that they had been routed only by a few blank cartridges – that six-pennyworth of powder had defeated them.

They were marched off to the town jail, guarded by the military, who now probably fancied that their night's work was over, and that the most turbulent and troublesome spirits in the town had been secured.

Such was not the case; however, for no sooner had comparative order been restored than common observation pointed to a dull red glare in the southern sky.

In a few more minutes there came in stragglers from the open country, shouting, "Fire! Fire!" with all their might.

Chapter 50
The Mob's Arrival at Sir Francis Varney's – The Attempt to Gain Admission

All eyes now turned towards the lightening southern sky; each moment it became more and more lurid with red and orange flickering lights which told of a blaze, which, if it was not extensive, was at all events raging fiercely.

There came too, upon the wind which set from that direction, strange sounds which resembled shouts of triumph, combined occasionally with sharper cries which could be indicative of alarm.

The attack had been made so carefully and so quietly upon the house of Sir Francis Varney that no one who had not actually accompanied the expedition was in the least aware that it had been undertaken, or that anything of the kind was on the agenda.

Now, however, it could no longer be kept a secret, and as the infuriated mob who had sought this flagrant means of giving vent to their anger, saw the flames from the blazing house rising high in the heavens, they felt convinced that further secrecy was out of the question.

Accordingly, in such cries and shouts as they would have indulged in from the very first had caution not been necessary, they now gave utterance to their feelings regarding the man whose destruction was aimed at.

"Death to the vampyre! – Death to the vampyre!" was the principal shout which echoed on the night sky, and it was uttered in tones which sounded like those of rage and disappointment.

It is necessary, now that we have disposed of the smaller number of rioters who committed so serious an outrage at the inn, that we should with some degree of method follow the proceedings of the larger number who ventured from the town towards Sir Francis Varney's.

These persons either had information of a very convincing nature, or a very strong suspicion that, notwithstanding the mysterious and most unaccountable disappearance of the vampyre in the old ruin, he would now be found, as usual, at his own residence.

Perhaps one of his own servants may have played the traitor to him, but however it was that it came about, there was certainly an air of confidence about some of the leaders of the tumultuous assemblage that induced a general belief that this time, at least, the vampyre would not escape popular vengeance for being what he was.

We have already noticed that these people went out of the town from different points, and did not assemble into one mass until they were at a sufficient distance from the town to be free from all fear of observation.

Then some of the less observant and cautious of them began to indulge in shouts of rage and defiance, but those who placed themselves foremost succeeded in procuring a halt, and one said, "Good friends, if we make any noise, it can only have one effect, and that is warning Sir Francis Varney and enabling him to escape. Therefore, if we cannot go on quietly, I propose that we return to our homes for we shall accomplish nothing."

This advice was sufficiently reasonable to meet with no dissension; a death-like stillness ensued which was only broken by an occasional group of two or three persons saying, in subdued tones, "That's right — that's right. Nobody speak."

"Come on, then," said the man who had given such judicious counsel, and the dark mass of men moved towards Sir Francis Varney's house as quietly as it was possible for such an assemblage to proceed.

Indeed, except for the sound of the footsteps, nothing could be heard of the mob at all, and that regular tramp, tramp, tramp, would have puzzled any one listening to it from any distance to know in which direction it was proceeding.

In this way they went on until Sir Francis Varney's house was reached, and even then a whispered word to halt was given, and all eyes were bent upon the building.

A light shone out from only one window out of the numerous ones with which the front of the mansion was studded, and from that there came rather an uncommonly bright reflection, probably arising from a reading lamp placed close to the window.

A general impression, although they could not have expressed exactly why, seemed to pervade everybody, that in the room from whence streamed that bright light was Sir Francis Varney.

"The vampyre's room!" said several. "The vampyre's room! That is it!"

"Yes," said he who had a kind of moral control over his comrades; "I have no doubt but he is there."

"What's to be done?" asked several.

"Make no noise whatever, but stand aside, so as not to be seen from the door when it is opened."

There was the mutter of general agreement to this advice.

"I will knock for admittance, and the moment it is answered, I will place this stick in such a manner within that the door cannot be closed again. Upon my saying 'Advance,' you will make a rush forward, and we shall have possession immediately of the house."

All this was agreed to. The mob shrunk close to the walls of the house, and out of immediate observation from the hall door or from any of the windows, and then the leader advanced, and knocked loudly for admission.

The silence was now of the most complete character that could be imagined. Those who came there so bent upon vengeance were thoroughly convinced of the necessity of extreme caution to save themselves even yet from being completely foiled.

They had abundant faith, from experience, of the resources in the way of escape of Sir Francis Varney, and not one among them was there who considered that there was any chance of capturing him, except by surprise, and when once they got hold of him, they determined he should not easily slip through their fingers.

The knock for admission produced no effect, and after waiting three or four minutes, it was very provoking to find such a wonderful amount of caution and cunning completely thrown away.

"Try again," whispered one.

"Have patience; I am going to try again."

The man had the ponderous old-fashioned knocker in his hand, and was about to make another appeal to Sir Francis Varney's door, when a strange voice said, "Perhaps you may as well say at once what you want, instead of knocking there to no purpose."

He gave a start, for the voice seemed to come from the very door itself.

Yet it sounded decidedly human, and upon a closer inspection, it was seen that a little wicket-gate, not larger than a man's face, had been opened from within.

This was terribly provoking. Here was an extent of caution on the part of the garrison quite unexpected. What was to be done?

"Well?" asked the man who appeared at the little opening.

"Oh," stammered he who had knocked; "I... "

"Well?"

"I – that is to say – ahem! Is Sir Francis Varney within?"

"Well?"

"I say, is Sir Francis Varney within?"

"Well; you have said it!"

"Ah, but you have not answered it."

"No."

"Well, is he at home?"

"I decline saying; so you had better, all of you, go back to the town again, for we are well provided with all material to resist any attack you may be fools enough to make." As he spoke, the servant shut the little square door with a bang that made his questioner jump again.

Here was a dilemma!

Chapter 51
The Attack Upon the Vampyre's House – The Fury of the Attack – The Forcing of the Doors, and the Struggle

A council of war was now called among the belligerents, who were somewhat taken aback by the steady refusal of the servant to admit them. They were surprised by the inhabitants' apparent determination to resist all endeavors on the part of the mob to get into and obtain possession of the house. It suggested that the inhabitants of the house were prepared to resist all attempts, and it would cost a few lives to get into the vampyre's house. This passed through the minds of many as they retired behind the angle of the wall where the council was to be held.

Once they were in their meeting place they looked in each others' faces as if to gather from each other's expressions the general tone of the feelings of their companions, but here they saw nothing that intimated the least idea of going back as they came.

"It's all very well, mates, to take care of ourselves, you know," began one tall, brawny fellow; "but, if we bean't to be sucked to death by a vampyre, why we must have the life out of him."

There was a general muttering of, "Ay, so we must."

"Jack Hodge is right; we must kill him, and there's no sin in it, for he has no right to it; he's robbed some poor fellow of his life to prolong his own."

"Ay, ay, that's the way he does; bring him out, I say, then see what we will do with him."

"Yes, catch him first," said one, "and then we can dispose of him afterwards. I say, neighbors, don't you think it would be as well to catch him first?"

"Well, what's to be done?" asked one; "here we are in a fix, I think, and I can't see our way out very clearly."

"I wish we could get in."

"But how this is to be accomplished is a thing I don't very well see the answer to," said a large specimen of humanity.

"The best thing that can be done will be to go round and look over the whole house, and then we may come upon some part where it is far easier to get in at than by the front door."

"But it won't do for us all to go round that way," said one; "a small party only should go, else they will have all their people stationed at one point, and if we can divide them, we shall beat them because they have not enough people to defend more than one point at a time; now we are numerous enough to make several attacks."

"Oh! That's the way to bother them all round; they'll give in, and then the place is our own."

"No, no," disagreed the big countryman, "I like to make a good rush and drive all afore us; you know what ye have to do then, and you do it, ye know."

"If you can."

"Ay, to be sure, if we can, as you say, but can't we? That's what I want to know."

"To be sure we can."

"Then we'll do it, mate – that's my mind; we'll do it. Come on, and let's have another look at the street-door."

The big countryman left the main body, and resolutely walked up to the main avenue, and approached the door, accompanied by about a dozen or less of the mob. When they came to the door, they commenced knocking and kicking most violently, and assailing it with all kinds of things they could lay their hands upon.

They continued at this violent exercise for some time – perhaps for five minutes, when the little square hole in the door was again opened, and a voice was heard to say, "You had better cease that kind of annoyance."

"We want to get in."

"It will cost you more lives to do so than you can afford to spare. We are well armed, and are prepared to resist any effort you can make."

"Oh! It's all very well, but, if you won't open, why we'll make you; that's all about it."

This was said as the big countryman and his companions were leaving the avenue towards the rest of the body.

"Then, takes this, as an earnest of what is to follow," said the man, and he discharged the contents of a blunderbuss through the small opening, and its report sounded to the rest of the mob like the report of a field-piece.

Fortunately for the party moving away from the door, the man couldn't take any aim, else it is questionable how many of the party would have got off unwounded. As it was, several of them found stray slugs were lodged in various parts of their persons, and it accelerated their retreat from the house of the vampyre.

"What luck?" inquired one of the mob to the others, as they came back; "I'm afraid you had the entire honor."

"Ay, ay, we have, and all the lead too," replied a man, as he placed his hand upon a sore part of his person, which bled in consequence of a wound.

"Well, what's to be done?"

"Danged if I know," said another.

"Give it up?" another suggested..

"No, no; have him out. I'll never give in while I can use a stick. They are in earnest and so are we. Don't let us be frightened because they have a gun or two – they can't have many, and besides, if they have, we are too many for them. Besides, we shall all die in our beds if we don't take care of the vampyre."

"Hurrah! Down with the vampyre!"

"So say I, lads. I don't want to be sucked to death when I'm a-bed. Better die like a man than such a dog's death as that, and you can have no revenge then."

"No, no; he has the better of us then. We'll have him out – we'll burn him – that's the way we'll do it."

"Ay, so we will; only let us get in."

The Flight Of The Vampyre

At that moment a chosen party returned who had been round the house to make a reconnaissance.

"Well, well," inquired the mob, "what can be done now – where can we get in?"

"In several places."

"All right; come along then; the place is our own."

"Stop a minute; they are armed at all points, and we must make an attack on all points, else we may fail. A party must go round to the front-door and attempt to beat it in; there are plenty of poles and things that could be used for such a purpose."

"There is, besides the front door, a garden-door, that opens into the house – a kind of parlor; a kitchen-door; a window in the flower-garden, and an entrance into a store-room; this place appears strong, and is therefore unguarded."

"The very point at which to make an attack."

"Not quite."

"Why not?"

"Because it can easily be defended, and rendered useless to us. We must make an attack upon all places but that, and, while they are being at those points, we can then enter at that place, and then you will find them desert the other places when they see us inside."

"Hurrah! Down with the vampyre!" cried the mob, as they listened to this advice, and appreciated the plan.

"Down with the vampyre!"

"Now then lads, divide, and make the attack; never mind their guns, they have but very few, and if you rush in upon them, you will soon have the guns yourselves."

"Hurrah! Hurrah!" shouted the mob.

The mob now moved away in different bodies, each strong enough to carry the house. They seized upon a variety of poles and stones, and then made for the various doors and windows that were pointed out by those who had made the discovery. Each one of those who had formed the party of observation formed a leader to the others, and at once proceeded to the post assigned him.

The attack was so sudden and so simultaneous that the servants were unprepared, and though they ran to the doors and fired away, still they did little good, for the doors were soon forced open by the enraged rioters, who proceeded in a much more systematic operation, using long heavy pieces of timber which were carried on the shoulder of several men, and driving with the force of battering-rams – which, in fact, they were – against the door.

Bang went the battering-ram, crash went the door, and the whole party rushed headlong in, carried forward by their own momentum and fell prostrate, battering ram and all, into the passage.

"Now, then, we have them," exclaimed the servants, who began to beat the whole party with blows, with every weapon they could secure.

The fallen men shouted loudly for assistance, but except for their fellows who came rushing in behind, they would have had but a sorry time of it.

"Hurrah!" shouted the mob; "the house is our own."

"Not yet," shouted the servants.

"We'll try," said the mob, and they rushed forward to drive the servants back; they met with a stout resistance, and as some of them had choppers and swords, there were a few wounds given, and presently bang went the blunderbuss.

Two or three of the mob reeled and fell.

This produced a momentary panic, and the servants then had the whole of the victory to themselves, and were about to charge, and clear the passage of their enemies, when a shout behind attracted their attention.

That shout was caused by an entrance being gained in another quarter, whence the servants were flying, and all was disorder.

"Hurrah! Hurrah!" shouted the mob.

The servants retreated to the stairs and here united; they made a stand, resolving to resist the whole force of the rioters, and they succeeded in doing so, too, for some minutes; blows were given and taken of a desperate character on both sides of the fray.

Somehow there were no deadly blows received by the servants; they were being forced and beaten, but they lost no life; this may be accounted for by the fact that the mob used no more deadly weapons than sticks.

The servants of Sir Francis Varney, on the contrary, were mostly armed with deadly weapons, which, however, they did not use unnecessarily.

They stood upon the hall steps – the grand staircase, with long poles or sticks, about the size of quarter-staves, and with these they belabored those below most unmercifully. Certainly, the mob were by no means cowards, for the struggle to close with their enemies was as great as ever, and as firm as could well be. Indeed, they rushed on with the desperation truly characteristic of honest men, and defied the heaviest blows, for as fast as one was stricken down another occupied his place and they insensibly pressed their close and compact front upon the servants, who were becoming fatigued and harassed.

"Fire, again," exclaimed a voice from among the servants. The mob made no retrograde movement, but still continued to press onwards, and in another moment a loud report rang through the house, and a smoke hung over the heads of the mob.

A long groan or two escaped some of the men who had been wounded, and still louder from those who had not been wounded a cry arose of, "Down with the vampyre – pull down – destroy and burn the whole place – down with them all."

A rush succeeded, and a few more discharges took place, when a shout above attracted the attention of both parties engaged in this fierce struggle. They paused by mutual consent, to look and see what was the cause of that shout.

Chapter 52
The Interview Between the Mob and Sir Francis Varney – The Mysterious Disappearance – The Wine Cellar

The shout that had so discomposed the parties who were thus engaged in a terrible struggle came from a party above.

"Hurrah! Hurrah!" they shouted a number of times, in a wild strain of delight. "Hurrah! Hurrah! Hurrah!"

The fact was, a party of the mob had clambered up a verandah and entered some of the rooms upstairs, whence they emerged just above the landing near the spot where the servants were resisting in a mass the efforts of the mob.

"Hurrah!" shouted the mob below.

"Hurrah!" shouted the mob above.

There was a momentary pause as the servants divided themselves into two bodies, and one turned to face those above, and the other those who were below.

A simultaneous shout was given by both parties of the mob, and a sudden rush was made by both bodies, and the servants of Sir Francis Varney were broken in an instant. They were instantly separated, and knocked about a good bit, but they were left to shift for themselves; the mob had a more important object in view which was lucky for the servants.

"Down with the vampyre!" they shouted. "Down with the vampyre!" And they rushed helter-skelter through the rooms until they came to one where the door was partially open, and they could see some person seated reading from a book.

"Here he is," they cried.

"Who? who?"

"The vampire."

"Down with him! Kill him! Burn him!"

"Hurrah! down with the vampire!"

These sounds were shouted out by a score of voices, and they rushed headlong into the room. But here their violence and headlong rush was suddenly restrained by the imposing and quiet appearance of the individual who was there seated.

The mob entered the room, and there was a sight, that if it did not astonish them, at least it caused them to pause before the individual who was seated there.

The room was filled with furniture, and a curtain was drawn across the room, and about the middle of it there stood a table, behind which sat Sir Francis Varney himself, looking all smiles and courtesy.

"Well, dang my smock-frock!" said one, "who'd ha' thought of this? He don't seem to care much about it."

"Well, I'm damned!" said another; "he seems pretty easy, at all events. What is he going to do?"

"Gentlemen," said Sir Francis Varney, rising with the blandest of smiles, "pray, gentlemen, permit me to inquire the cause of this condescension on your part. The visit is kind."

The mob looked at Sir Francis, and then at each other, and then at Sir Francis again, but nobody spoke. They were awed by this gentlemanly and his composed behavior.

"If you honor me with this visit from pure affection and neighborly good-will, I thank you."

"Down with the vampyre!" said one, who was concealed behind the rest, and not so much overawed as he had not seen Sir Francis.

Sir Francis Varney rose to his full height; a light gleamed across his features; they were strongly defined then. His long front teeth, too, showed most strongly when he smiled, as he did now, and said, in a

The Flight Of The Vampyre

bland voice, "Gentlemen, I am at your service. Permit me to say you are all welcome to all I can do for you. I fear the interview will be somewhat inconvenient and unpleasant to you. As for myself, I am entirely at your service."

As Sir Francis spoke, he bowed, and folded his hands together, and stepped forwards, but, instead of coming onwards to them, he walked behind the curtain and was immediately hidden from their view.

"Down with the vampyre!" shouted one.

"Down with the vampyre!" rang through the apartment, and the mob now, not awed by the coolness and courtesy of Sir Francis, rushed forward, and overturning the table tore down the curtain to the floor, but to their amazement there was no Sir Francis Varney present.

"Where is he?"

"Where is the vampyre?"

"Where has he gone?"

These were cries that escaped everyone's lips, and yet no one could give an answer to them.

Sir Francis Varney simply was not there. They were completely thunderstruck. They could not find out where he had gone to. There was no possible means of escape that they could perceive. There was not an odd corner, or even anything that could, by any possibility, give even a suspicion that even a temporary concealment could take place.

They looked over every inch of flooring and of wainscoting; not the remotest trace could be discovered of either Sir Francis Varney or his hiding place.

"Where is he?" one asked.

"I don't know," answered another. "I can't see where he could have gone. There ain't a hole as big as a keyhole."

"My eye!" said one; "I shouldn't be at all surprised, if he were to blow up the whole house."

"You don't say so!"

"I never heard as how vampyres could do so much as that. They ain't the sort of people," said another.

"But if they can do one thing, they can do another."

"That's very true."

"And what's more, I never heard as how a vampyre could make himself into nothing before, yet he has done so."

"He may be in this room now."

"He may."

- 65 -

"My eyes! what precious long teeth he had!"

"Yes, and had he fixed one of 'em into your arm, he would have drawn every drop of blood out of your body; you may depend upon that," said an old man.

"He was very tall."

"Yes; too tall to be any good."

"I shouldn't like him to have laid hold of me, though, tall as he is, and then he would have lifted me up high enough to break my neck when he let me fall."

The mob rooted about the room; they tore everything out of its place, and as the object of their search seemed to be far enough beyond their reach, their courage rose in proportion, and they shouted and screamed with a proportionate increase of noise and bustle. Every hole and corner of the house was searched, but there was no Sir Francis Varney to be found.

"The cellars, the cellars!" shouted a voice.

"The cellars, the cellars!" re-echoed nearly every pair of lips in the whole place; in another moment, there was crushing and crowding to get down into the cellars.

"Hurray!" said one, as he knocked off the neck of the bottle that first came to hand. "Here's luck to vampyre-hunting! Success to our chase!" And he took a long swig of the bottle's contents.

"So say I, neighbor, but is that your manners to drink before your betters?"

So saying, the speaker knocked the other's elbow while he was in the act of lifting the wine to his mouth, and thus he upset it over his face and eyes.

"Damn it!" cried the man; "how it makes my eyes smart! Dang you! If I could see, I'd wring your neck!"

"Success to vampyre-hunting!" shouted one.

"May we be lucky yet!" exclaimed another.

"I wouldn't be luckier than this," said another, as he, too, emptied a bottle. "We couldn't desire better entertainment, where the reckoning is all paid."

"Capital wine this!"

"I say, Huggins!"

"Well," said Huggins.

"What are you drinking?"

"Wine."

The Flight Of The Vampyre

"What wine?"

"Danged if I know," was the reply. "It's wine, I suppose, for I know it ain't beer nor spirits; so it must be wine."

"Are you sure it ain't bottled men's blood?"

"Eh?"

"Bottled blood, man! Who knows what a vampyre drinks? It may be his wine. He may feast upon that before he goes to bed of a night, drink anybody's health, and make himself cheerful on bottled blood!"

"Oh, danged! I'm so sick; I wish I hadn't taken the stuff. It may be as you say, neighbor, and then we be cannibals."

"Or vampyres."

"There's a pretty thing to think of."

By this time some were drunk, some were partially drunk, and the remainder were crowding into the cellars to get their share of the wine. The servants had now slunk away unnoticed by the rioters, who, having nobody to oppose them, no longer thought of anything save the searching after the vampyre, and the destruction of the property. A considerable time had soon been spent in this manner, and yet they could not find the object of their search.

There was not a room, or cupboard, or a cellar, that was capable of containing a cat that they did not search, besides a part of the rioters keeping a very strict watch on the outside of the house and all about the grounds, to prevent the possibility of the escape of the vampyre.

There was a general cessation of active hostilities at that moment; a reaction after the violent excitement and exertion they had made to get in. Then the escape of their victim, and the mysterious manner in which he got away, was also a cause of the reaction, and the rioters looked in each others' countenances inquiringly.

Above all, the discovery of the wine-cellar tended to withdraw them from violent measures, but this could not last long; there must be an end to such a scene, for there never was a large body of men assembled for an evil purpose who were, for any length of time, peaceable.

To prevent the more alarming effects of drunkenness, some few of the rioters, after having taken some small portion of the wine, became from the peculiar flavor it possessed, imbued with the idea that it was really blood, and forthwith commenced an instant attack upon the wine and liquors, and they were soon mingling in one stream throughout the cellars.

This destruction was loudly declaimed against by the large portion of the rioters, who were drinking, but before they could make any efforts to save the liquor, the work of destruction had not only been begun, but was ended, and the consequence was that the cellars were very soon evacuated by the mob.

Chapter 53
The Destruction of Sir Francis Varney's House by Fire – The Arrival of the Military, and a Second Mob

Thus many moments had not elapsed before the feelings of the rioters were directed into a different channel from that in which it had so lately flowed. When searching around the house and grounds for the vampyre, they became impatient and angry at not finding him. Many believed that he was still hidden somewhere within the house, while many were of the opinion that he had flown away by some mysterious means only possessed by vampyres and such-like people.

"Set fire to the house, and burn him out," suggested one.

Soon the shouts of, "Fire the house! Burn the den!" arose from many of those persons present, and then the mob was again animated by the love of mischief that seemed to be the strongest feelings that animated them.

"Burn him out – burn him out!" were the only words that could be heard from any of the mob. The words ran through the house like wild-fire; nobody thought of anything else, and all were seen milling around in confusion. There was no lack of good will on the part of the mob to the undertaking; far from it, and they proceeded in the work enthusiastically. They worked together with good will, and the result was soon seen by the heaps of combustible materials that were collected in a short time from all parts of the house.

All the old dry wood furniture that could be found was piled up in a heap, and to these were added a number of small logs, and also some wood-shavings that were found in the cellar.

"All right!" exclaimed one man, in exultation.

"Yes," replied a second; "all right – all right! Set light to it, and he will be smoked out if he is not burned."

"Let us be sure that we are all out of the house," suggested one of the bystanders.

"Ay, ay," shouted several; "give them all a chance. Search through the house and give them a warning."

"Very well; give me the light, and then when I come back, I will set light to the fire at once, and then I shall know all is empty, and so will you too."

This was at once agreed to by everyone, and the light being handed to the man, he ascended the stairs, crying out in a loud voice, "Come out – come out! The house is on fire!"

"Fire! Fire! Fire!" shouted the mob as a chorus at intervals.

In about ten minutes more, there came a cry of, "All right; the house is empty," from up the stairs, and the man descended in haste to the hall.

"Make haste, lads, and fire away, for I see the red coats are leaving the town."

"Hurrah! Hurrah!" shouted the infuriated mob. "Fire – fire – fire the house! Burn out the vampyre! Burn down the house – burn him out, and see if he can stand fire."

Amidst all this tumult there came a sudden blaze, for the pile had been set fire to.

"Hurrah!" shouted the mob – "Hurrah!" and they danced like maniacs round the fire; looking, in fact, like they were possessed, dancing round their roasting victims like some demons at an infernal feast.

The fire had been started at twenty different places, and the flames united into one, and suddenly shot up with a velocity, and roared with a sound that caused many who were present to make a precipitate retreat from the hall. This soon became a necessary measure of self-preservation, and it required no urging to induce them to quit a place that was burning rapidly and furiously.

"Get the poles and firewood," shouted some of the mob, and, lo, it was done almost by magic. They brought the small sticks and wood piled up for winter use, and laid them near all the doors, and especially near the main entrance. Soon every gate or door belonging to the outhouses was brought forward and placed upon the fire, which now began to reach the upper stories.

"Hurrah – fire! Hurrah – fire!" rose as a loud shout of triumph from the mob as they viewed the progress of the flames roaring and tearing through the house doors and the windows.

The Flight Of The Vampyre

Each new victory of the element was a signal to the mob for a cheer, and a hearty cheer, too, erupted from them.

"Where is the vampyre now?" exclaimed one in triumphant tones.

"Ha! Where is he?" asked another smugly.

"If he be there," said the man, pointing to the flames, "I reckon he's got a warm berth of it, and, at the same time, very little water to boil in his kettle."

"Ha, ha! What a funny old man is Bob Mason; he's always poking fun; he'd joke if his wife were dying."

"There is many a true word spoken in jest," suggested another; "and, to my mind, Bob Mason wouldn't be very much grieved if his wife were to die."

"Die?" said Bob; "she and I have lived and quarreled daily for a matter of five-and-thirty years, and, if that ain't enough to make a man sick of being married, and of his wife, hang me, that's all. I say I am tired." This was said with much apparent sincerity, and several laughed at the old man's heartiness.

"It's all very well," said the old man; "it's all very well to laugh about matters you don't understand, but I know it isn't a joke – not a bit on it. I tell you what it is, neighbor, I never made but one grand mistake in all my life."

"And what was that?"

"To tie myself to a woman."

"Why, you'd get married to-morrow if your wife were to die today," one of his mates told him.

"If I did, I hope I may marry a vampyre. I should have something then to think about. I should know what's o'clock. But, as for my old woman, lord, lord, I wish Sir Francis Varney had had her for life. I'll warrant when the next natural term of his existence came round again, he wouldn't be in no hurry to renew it; if he did, I should say that vampyres had the happy lot of managing women, which I haven't got."

"No, nor anybody else," one said, to general laughing agreement.

A loud shout now attracted their attention, and upon looking in the quarter whence it came, they observed a large body of people coming towards them; from one end of the mob could be seen a long string of red coats.

"The red coats!" shouted one.

"The military!" shouted another.

The Flight Of The Vampyre

It was plain the military who had been placed in the town to quell disturbances had been made acquainted with the proceedings at Sir Francis Varney's house, and were now marching to relieve the place, and to save the property.

They were, as we have stated, accompanied by a vast concourse of people who came out to see what they were going to see, and seeing the flames at Sir Francis Varney's house, they determined to come all the way, and be present for whatever happened next.

The military, seeing the disturbance in the distance and the flames issuing from the windows, made the best of their way towards the scene of tumult with what speed they could make.

"Here they come," said one.

"Yes, just in time to see what is done."

"Yes, they can go back and say we have burned the vampire's house down – hurrah!"

"Hurrah!" shouted the mob, in prolonged accents, and it reached the ears of the military.

The officer urged the men onwards, and they responded to his words by exerting themselves to step out a little faster.

"Oh, they should have been here before this; it's no use, now, they are too late."

"Yes, they are too late."

"I wonder if the vampyre can breathe through the smoke, and live in fire," speculated one.

"I should think he must be able to do so if he can stand shooting as we know he can – you can't kill a vampyre, but yet he must be consumed if the fire actually touches him."

"Hurrah!" shouted the mob as a tall flame shot through the top windows of the house.

The fire had got the ascendant now, and no hopes could be entertained, however extravagant, of saving the smallest article that had been left in the mansion.

"Hurrah!" shouted the mob with the military.

"Hurrah!" shouted the others in reply.

"Quick march!" said the officer, and then in a loud, commanding tone, he shouted, "Clear the way, there! Clear the way."

"Ay, there's room enough for you," said old Mason; "what are you making so much noise about?"

The Flight Of The Vampyre

There was a general laugh at the officer, who took no notice of the words, but ordered his men up before the burning pile, which was now an immense mass of flame.

The mob who had accompanied the military now mingled with the mob that had set the house of Sir Francis Varney on fire before the military had caught up with them.

"Halt!" cried the officer, and the men, obedient to the word of command, halted, and drew up in a double line before the house.

There were then some words of command issued, and some more given to some of the subalterns, and a party of men under the command of a sergeant was sent off from the main body to make a circuit of the house and grounds.

The officer gazed for some moments upon the burning pile without speaking, and then, turning to the next in command, he said in low tones as he looked upon the mob, "We have come too late."

"Yes, much."

"The house is now nearly gutted."

"It is."

"And those who came crowding along with us are inextricably mingled with the others who have been the cause of all this mischief; there's no distinguishing them one from another."

"And if you did, you could not say who had done it, and who had not; you could prove nothing."

"Exactly," he agreed angrily.

"I shall not attempt to take prisoners, unless any act is perpetrated beyond what has been done."

"This has been a night of singular affairs."

"Very."

"This Sir Francis Varney is represented to be a courteous, gentlemanly man," said the officer.

"No doubt about it, but he's beset by a parcel of people who do not mind cutting a throat if they can get an opportunity of doing so."

"And I expect they will."

"Yes, when there is a popular excitement against any man, he had better leave this part of the country at once and altogether. It is dangerous to tamper with popular prejudices; no man who has any value for his life ought to do so. It is a sheer act of suicide.

Chapter 54
The Burning of Varney's House – A Night Scene – Popular Superstition

The officer ceased to speak, and then the parties whom he had sent around the house and those sent to check the grounds returned, and the sergeant went forward to make his report to his superior officer.

After the usual salutation, he waited for the inquiry to be put to him as to what he had seen.

"Well, Scott, what have you done?"

"I went round the premises, sir, according to your instructions, but saw no one either in the vicinity of the house, or in the grounds around it."

"No strangers, eh?"

"No, sir, none."

"You saw nothing at all likely to lead to any knowledge as to who it was that has caused this catastrophe?"

"No, sir."

"Have you learnt anything among the people who are the perpetrators of this fire?"

"No, sir."

"Well, then, that will do, unless there is anything else that you can think of."

"Nothing further, sir, unless it is that I heard some of them say that Sir Francis Varney has perished in the flames."

"Good heavens!"

"So I heard, sir."

"That must be impossible; he must have seen the flames and gotten out, and yet why should it be so? Go back, Scott, and bring me some person who can give me some information upon this point."

The sergeant moved towards the people, who looked at him without any distrust for he came single-handed, and they thought he came with the intention of learning what they knew of each other, and so strolled about with the intention of getting up accusations against them. But this was not the case; the officer didn't like his employment well enough; he'd rather have been elsewhere.

At length the sergeant came to one man, whom he accosted, and asked him, "Do you know anything of yonder fire?"

"Yes; I do know it is a fire."

"Yes, and so do I."

"My friend," said the sergeant, "when a soldier asks a question he does not expect an uncivil answer."

"But a soldier may ask a question that may have an uncivil end to it," responded the man who thought himself something of a wit.

"He may, but it is easy to say so."

"I do say so, then, now."

"Then I'll not trouble you anymore."

The sergeant moved on a pace or two more, and then, turning to the mob, he bellowed to be heard over the clamor, "Is there any one among you who can tell me anything concerning the fate of Sir Francis Varney?"

"Burnt!"

"Did you see him burn?"

"No, but I saw him."

"In the flames?"

"No; before the house was on fire."

"In the house?"

"Yes, and he has not been seen to leave it since, and we conclude he must have been burned."

"Will you come and say as much to my commanding officer? It is all I want."

"Shall I be detained?"

"No."

"Then I will go," answered the man, and he hobbled out of the crowd towards the sergeant. "I will go and see the officer and tell him what I know, and that is very little and can prejudice no one."

"Hurrah!" said the crowd, when they heard this latter assertion, for at first they began to be in some alarm lest there should be something wrong about this, and some of them get identified as being active in the fray.

The sergeant led the man back to the spot where the officer stood a little way in advance of his men.

"Well, Scott," he said, "what have we here?"

"A man who has volunteered a statement, sir."

"Oh! Well, my man, can you say anything concerning all this disturbance that we have here?"

"No, sir."

"Then what did you come here for?"

"I understood the Sergeant wanted someone who could speak of Sir Francis Varney."

"Well?"

"I saw him."

"Where?"

"In the house.

"Exactly, but have you not seen him out of it?"

"Not since, nor has anyone else, I believe."

"Where was he?"

"Upstairs, where he suddenly disappeared, and nobody can tell where he may have gone to. But he has not been seen out of the house since, and they say he could not have gone bodily out without someone having seen him."

"He must have been burnt," mused the officer; "he could not escape, one would imagine, without being seen by some one out of such a mob."

"Oh, dear no, for I am told they placed a watch at every hole, window, or door, however high, and they saw nothing of him – he did not even fly out!"

"Fly out! I'm speaking of a man!"

"And I of a vampire!" said the man carelessly.

"A vampyre! Pooh, pooh!"

"Oh no! Sir Francis Varney is a vampyre! There can be no doubt about it. You only have to look at him, and you will be satisfied of that. See his great sharp teeth in front, and ask yourself what they are for, and you will soon find the answer. They are to make holes in the bodies of his victims through which he can suck their blood!"

The officer looked at the man in astonishment for a few moments, as if he doubted his own ears, and then he asked, "Are you serious?"

"I am ready to swear to it."

"Well, I have heard a great deal about this popular superstition, and thought I had seen something of it, but this is decidedly the worst case that ever I saw or heard. You had better go home, my man, than by your presence countenance such a gross absurdity."

"For all that," said the man, "Sir Francis Varney is a vampyre – a blood-sucker – a human blood-sucker!"

"Get away with you," ordered the officer, "and do not repeat such folly before anyone."

The man almost jumped when he heard the tone in which this was spoken, for the officer was both angry and contemptuous.

"These people," he added, turning to the sergeant, "are ignorant in the extreme. One would think we had got into the country of vampires instead of into a civilized community."

With the fire providing the only light, the darkness of night was still fast closing around them. The mob stood a motley mass of human beings, wedged together, dark and somber, gazing upon the mischief that had been done – the work of their hands. The military stood at ease before the burning pile, and by their order and regularity presented a contrast to the mob, as strongly by their bright gleaming arms as by their dress and order.

The flames now enveloped the whole mansion. There was not a window or a door from which the fiery element did not burst forth in clouds, and forked flames came rushing forth with a velocity truly wonderful.

The countryside was enveloped in darkness, and the burning house could be seen for miles around. It formed a rallying-point to all men's eyes.

The fire-engines that were within reach came tearing across the country, and came to the fire, but they were of no avail. There was no supply of water, save from the ornamental ponds. These they could only get at by means that were tedious and unsatisfactory, considering the emergency of the case.

The house was a lonely one, and it was being entirely consumed before they arrived, and therefore there was not the remotest chance of saving the least article.

Thus the men stood idly by, passing their remarks upon the fire and the mob.

Those who stood around, within the influence of the red glare of the flames, looked like demons in the infernal regions watching the progress of the fire, which we are told by good Christians is the doom of the unfortunate in spirit, and the woefully unlucky in circumstances.

It was a strange sight, and there were many persons who would, without doubt, have rather been snug by their own fire-side than they would have remained there, but it happened that no one felt inclined to express his inclination to his neighbor and; consequently, no one said anything on the subject.

No one would venture to go alone across the fields, where the spirit of the vampyre might, for all they knew to the contrary, be waiting to pounce upon them and worry them.

No, no; no man would have quitted that mob to go back alone to the village; they would sooner have stood there all night through. That was an alternative that none of the number would very willingly accept.

The hours passed away, and the house that had been that morning a noble and well-furnished mansion, was now a smoldering heap of ruins. The flames had become somewhat subdued, and there was now more smoke than flames. The fire had gradually exhausted itself. There was now no more material that could serve it for fuel, and the flames began to become gradually subdued.

Suddenly there was a rush, and then a bright flame shot upward for an instant, so bright and so strong that it threw a flash of light over the country for miles, but it was only momentary, and it subsided.

The roof, which had been built strong enough to resist almost anything, after burning for a considerable time suddenly gave way, and came in with a tremendous crash, and then all was for a moment darkness.

After this, the fire might be said to be subdued, having burned itself out. And the flames that could now be seen were only the result of so much charred wood that would probably smolder for a day or two if left to itself to do so. A dense mass of smoke arose from the ruins and blackened the atmosphere around, telling the spectators the work was done.

Chapter 55
The Return of the Mob and Military to the Town – The Madness of the Mob – The Grocer's Revenge

At the termination of the conflagration, or rather at the fall of the roof, with the loss of grandeur in the spectacle, men's minds began to be free from the excitement that chained them to the spot.

There now remained little more than the livid glare of the hot and burning embers, and this did not extend far, for the walls were too strongly built to fall in from their own weight; they were strong and stout and intercepted the little light the ashes would have given out.

The Flight Of The Vampyre

The mob now began to feel fatigued and chilly. It had been standing and walking about many hours, and the approach of exhaustion could not be put off much longer, especially since there was no longer any great excitement to combat its effects.

The officer, seeing that nothing was to be done, collected his men together, and they were soon seen in motion. He had been ordered to stop any tumult that he might have seen, and to save any property. But there was nothing to do now; all the property that could have been saved was now destroyed, and the mob was beginning to disperse and creep towards their own houses.

The order was then given for the men to take close order and keep together, and the word to march was given, which the men obeyed with alacrity, for they had no desire to stay there all night.

The return to the village of both the mob and the military was not without its trials; accidents of all kinds were rife amongst them; the military; however, taking the open paths, soon diminished the distance to the town with little or no accidents, save such as might have been expected from the state of the fields after they had been so much trodden down of late.

Not so the townspeople or the peasantry, for by way of keeping up their spirits and amusing themselves on their way home, they commenced larking, as they called it, which often meant the execution of practical jokes, and these sometimes were of a serious nature.

The night was dark at that hour, especially so when there were a number of persons wandering about, so that little or nothing could be seen of the track they were following. The mistakes and blunders that were made were numerous. In one place there were a number of people penetrating a path that lead only to a hedge and deep ditch; indeed, it was a brook very deep and muddy.

Here they came to a stop and endeavored to ascertain its width, but the little reflected light they had was deceptive, and it did not appear so broad as it was.

"Oh, I can jump it," exclaimed one.

"And so can I," said another, "I have done so before, and why should I not do so now."

This was unanswerable, and as there were many present, at least a dozen were eager to jump.

"If you can do it, I know I can," said a brawny countryman; "so I'll do it at once."

"The sooner the better," shouted someone behind, "or you'll have no room for a run, here's a lot of 'em coming up; jump over as quickly as you can."

Thus urged, the jumpers at once made a rush to the edge of the ditch, and many jumped, and many more, from the prevailing darkness, did not see exactly where the ditch was and taking one or two steps too many, found themselves in above their waists in muddy water.

Nor were those who jumped much better off, for nearly all jumped short or fell backwards into the stream. They needed to be dragged out; they were in a terrible state.

"Oh, lord! Oh, lord!" exclaimed one poor fellow, dripping wet and shivering with cold, "I shall die! oh, the rheumatiz; there'll be a pretty winter for me; I'm half dead."

"Hold your noise," said another, "and help me to get the mud out of my eye; I can't see."

"Never mind," added a third, "considering how you jump, I don't think you want to see."

"This comes of hunting vampyres."

"Oh, it's all a judgment; who knows but he may not be in the air; it is nothing to laugh at as I shouldn't be surprised if he were; only think how precious pleasant."

"However pleasant it may be to you," remarked one, "it's profitable to a good many."

"How so?"

"Why, see the numbers of things that will be spoiled; coats torn, hats crushed, heads broken, and shoes burst. Oh, it's an ill-wind that blows nobody any good."

"So it is, but you may benefit anybody you like, so you don't do it at my expense."

In one part of a field where there were some fences and gates, a big countryman caught a fat shopkeeper with the arms of the fence a terrible poke in the stomach; while the breath was knocked out of the poor man's stomach, and he was gasping with agony, the fellow set to laughing, started his companions, who were of the same class "I say, Jim, look at the grocer, he hasn't got any wind to spare, I'd run him for a wager, see how he gapes like a fish out of water."

The Flight Of The Vampyre

The poor shopkeeper felt indeed like a fish out of water, and as he afterwards declared he felt just as if he had had a red hot poker thrust into the midst of his stomach and there left to cool.

However, the grocer would be revenged upon his tormentor, who had now lost sight of him, but the fat man, after a time recovering his wind, and the pain in his stomach becoming less intense, he gathered himself up.

"My name ain't Jones," he muttered, "if I don't get my own back for that; I'll do something that shall make him remember what it is to insult a respectable tradesman. I'll never forgive such an insult. It is dark, and that's why it is he has dared to do this."

Filled with dire thoughts and a spirit of revenge, he looked from side to side to see what was useable to obtain his object, but could find nothing.

"It's shameful," he muttered; "what would I give for a little retort. I'd plaster his ugly countenance." As he spoke, he placed his hands on some fence posts to rest himself; soon he found that they stuck to them, the posts had been newly pitched that day. A bright idea now struck him.

"If I could only get a handful of this stuff," he thought, "I should be able to serve him out for serving me out. I will, cost what it may; I'm resolved upon that. I'll not have my wind knocked out and my inside set on fire for nothing. No, no; I'll be revenged on him."

With this view he felt over the posts, and found that he could scrape off a little only, but not with his hands; indeed, it only plastered them; he, therefore, marched about for something to scrape it off with.

"Ah, I have a knife, a large pocket knife, that will do, that is the sort of thing I want," he muttered to himself, remembering.

He immediately commenced feeling for his knife, but had scarcely got his hand into his pocket when he found there would be a great difficulty in either pushing it in further or withdrawing it altogether, for the pitch made it difficult to do either, and his pocket stuck to his hands like a glove.

"Damn it," said the grocer, "who would have thought of that! Here's a pretty go; curse that fellow! He is the cause of all this; I'll be revenged upon him, if it's a year hence."

The enraged grocer drew his hand out, but was unable to effect his object in withdrawing the knife also, but he saw something shining, he stooped to pick it up, exclaiming as he did so, in a gratified tone of voice,

"Ah, here's something that will do better." As he made a grasp at it, he found he had inserted his hand into something soft. "God bless me! What now?" And, pulling his hand hastily away, he found that it stuck slightly, and then he saw what it was.

"Ay, ay, the very thing. Surely it must have been placed here on purpose by the people."

The fact was, he had placed his hand into a pot of pitch that had been left by the people who had been at work at pitching the poles, but had been attracted by the fire at Sir Francis Varney's; they had left their work to observe the fire, and the pitch was left on a smoldering peat fire, so that when Mr. Jones, the grocer, accidentally put his hand into it he found it just warm.

When he made this discovery he dabbed his hand again into the pitch-pot, exclaiming, "In for a penny, in for a pound."

And he endeavored to secure as large a handful of the slippery and sticky stuff as he could, and after this done he set off to come up with the big countryman who had done him so much indignity and made his stomach uncomfortable.

He soon came up with him, for the man had stopped rather behind his close mates, and was larking, as it is called, with some men, to whom he was a companion.

He had slipped down a bank, and was partially sitting down on the soft mud. In his bustle, the little grocer came down with a slide, close to the big countryman.

"Ah – ah! my little grocer," said the countryman, holding out his hand to catch him, and drawing him towards himself, "You will come and sit down by the side of your old friend."

As he spoke, he endeavored to pull Mr. Jones down, too, but that individual only replied by fetching the countryman a swinging smack across the face with the handful of pitch.

"There, take that, and now we are quits; we shall be old friends after this, eh? Are you satisfied? You'll remember me, I'll warrant."

As the grocer spoke, he rubbed his hands over the face of the fallen man, and then rushed from the spot with all the haste he could make.

The countryman sat a moment or two confounded, cursing, and swearing, and spluttering, vowing vengeance, believing that it was mud only that had been plastered over his face, but when he put his hands up, and found out what it was, he roared and bellowed like a town-bull.

He cried out to his companions that his eyes were pitched, but they only laughed at him, thinking he was having some foolish lark with them.

It was next day before he got home after wandering about all night, and it took him a week to wash the pitch off by means of grease, and ever afterwards he recollected the pitching of his face, nor did he ever forget or forgive the grocer for playing him such a trick.

Thus it was the whole party returned a long while after dark across the fields, with all the various accidents that were likely to befall such a large assemblage of people.

The vampyre hunting cost many of them dear, for clothes were injured on all sides, hats lost, and shoes missing in a manner that put some of the rioters to much inconvenience. Soon afterwards, the military retired to their quarters, and the townspeople at length became tranquil, and nothing more was heard or done that night.

Chapter 56
The Departure of the Bannerworths from the Hall – The New Residence – Jack Pringle, Pilot

The same evening on which the house of Sir Francis Varney was burned down by the mob, another scene of a different character was enacted at Bannerworth Hall where the owners of that ancient place were departing from it. They were preparing for their departure.

The Admiral was walking up and down the lawn in front the house and looking up at the windows every now and then, and turning to Jack Pringle, he said, "Jack, you dog."

"Ay – ay sir."

"Mind you convoy these women into the right port; do you hear? And no mistaking the bearings; do you hear?"

"Ay, ay sir."

"These crafts want care, and you are pilot, commander, and all; so mind and keep your weather eye open."

"Ay, ay, sir. I knows the craft well enough, and I knows the roads, too."

The Flight Of The Vampyre

There was now someone moving within, and the Admiral, followed by Jack Pringle, entered the Hall. Henry Bannerworth was there. They were all ready to go when the coach which the Admiral had ordered for them finally arrived.

"Jack, you lubber; where are you?"

"Here I am, sir."

"Go and station yourself up in some place where you can keep a good look-out for the coach, and come and report when you see it."

"Ay – ay, sir," said Jack, and away he went from the room to station himself up in one of the trees that commanded a good view of the main road.

"Admiral Bell," said Henry, "here we are, trusting implicitly in you, and in doing so, I am sure I am doing right."

"You will see that," said the Admiral. "All's fair and honest as yet, and what is to come, will speak for itself."

"I hope you won't suffer from any of these nocturnal visits from the vampyre," said Henry.

"I don't much care about them, but old Admiral Bell don't strike his colors to an enemy, however ugly the enemy may look. No, no; it must be a better craft than his own that'll take him, and one who won't run away, but that will grapple yard-arm and yard-arm, you know."

"Why, Admiral, you must have seen many dangers in your time, and are used to all kinds of disturbances and conflicts. You have had a life of experience."

The Admiral was just beginning one of his long-winded stories, but as he spoke, Flora and her mother entered the apartment.

"Well, Admiral, we are all ready," Henry informed him."And though I may feel somewhat sorry at leaving the old Hall, yet it arises from attachment to the place, and not any disinclination to be beyond the reach of these dreadful alarms."

"And I, too, shall be by no means sorry," said Flora; "I am sure it is some gratification to know we leave a friend here, rather than the other who would have had the place, if he could have got it, by any means."

"Ah, that's true enough, Miss Flora," agreed the Admiral; "but we'll run the enemy down yet, depend upon it. But once away, you will be free from these terrors, and now, as you have promised, do not let yourselves be seen anywhere at all."

"You have our promises, Admiral, and they shall be religiously kept, I can assure you."

"Boat, ahoy – ahoy!" shouted Jack.

"What boat?" said the Admiral, surprised, and then he muttered, "Confound you for a lubber! Didn't I tell you to mind your bearings, you dog-fish you?"

"Ay, ay, sir, and so I did."

"You did."

"Yes, here they are. Squint over the larboard bulk-heads, as they call walls, and then between the two trees on the starboard side of the course, then straight ahead for a few hundred fathoms, when you come to a funnel as is smoking like the crater of Mount Vesuvius, and then in a line with that on the top of the hill, comes our boat."

"Well," said the Admiral, "that'll do. Now go open the gates; mind you keep a bright look out, and if you see anybody near your watch, why douse their glimmer."

"Ay – ay, sir," said Jack, and he disappeared.

"Rather a lucid description," said Henry, as he thought of Jack's report to the Admiral.

"Oh, it's a seaman's report. I know what he means; it's quicker and plainer than the land lingo to my ears, and Jack can't talk any other way, you see."

By this time the coach came into the yard, and the whole party descended into the court-yard, where they came to take leave of the old place.

"Farewell, Admiral," said Flora, embracing him precipitously.

"Good bye," said the Admiral. "I hope the place you are going to will be such as will please you – I hope it will."

"I am sure we shall endeavor to be pleased with it, and I am pretty sure we shall."

"Good bye."

"Farewell, Admiral Bell," said Henry.

"You remember your promises?"

"I do. Good bye, Mr. Chillingworth."

"Good bye," said Mr. Chillingworth, who came up to bid them farewell; "a pleasant journey, and may you all be the happier for it."

"Are you not coming with us?"

"No; I have some business of importance to attend to, else I should have the greatest pleasure in doing so. But good bye; we shall not be long apart, I dare say."

"I hope not," said Henry.

The door of the carriage was shut by the Admiral, who looked round, saying, "Jack – Jack Pringle, where are you, you dog?"

"Here am I," said Jack.

"You dog you; didn't I tell you to mind your bearings?"

"So I will," said Jack, "fore and aft – fore and aft, Admiral."

"You had better," said the Admiral, who relaxed into a broad grin which he concealed from Jack Pringle.

Jack mounted the coach-box, and away it went, just as it was getting dark. The old Admiral had locked up all the rooms in the presence of Henry Bannerworth, and when the coach had gone out of sight, Mr. Chillingworth came back to the Hall where he joined the Admiral.

"Well," he said, "they are gone Admiral Bell, and we are alone; we have a clear stage."

"The two things of all others I most desire. Now, they will be strangers where they are going to, and that will be something gained. I will endeavor to do something if I get yard-arm and yard-arm with these pirates. I'll make 'em feel the weight of true metal; I'll board 'em – damne, I'll do everything."

"Everything that can be done."

*****

"Ay – ay."

The coach which carried the Bannerworth family away continued its course without hindrance, and they met no one on their road during the whole drive. The fact was, nearly everybody was at the conflagration at Sir Francis Varney's house.

Flora did not know which way they were going, and after a time, all trace of the road was lost. Darkness set in, and they all sat in silence in the coach. After some time had been spent thus, Flora Bannerworth turned to Jack Pringle and asked, "Are we near, or have we much further to go?"

"Not very much, ma'am," said Jack. "All's right, however – ship in the direct course and no breakers ahead – no lookout necessary; however there's a landlubber aloft to keep a look out."

All this was not very well understood by them, but Jack seemed to have his own reasons for silence. They asked him no further questions, and in about three-quarters of an hour, during which time the coach had been driving through the trees, they came to a standstill by a sudden pull of the checkstring[xiv] from Jack, who said, "Hilloa! – take in sails, and drop anchor."

"Is this the place?" his companions enquired anxiously.

"Yes, here we are," said Jack; "we're in port now, at all events;" and he began to sing, "The trials and the dangers of the voyage is past," when the coach door opened, and they all got out and looked about them with great interest.

"Up the garden if you please, ma'am – as quick as you can; the night air is very cold."

Flora and her mother and brother took the hint, which was meant by Jack to mean that they were not to be seen outside. They at once entered a pretty garden, and then they came to a very neat and picturesque cottage. They had no time to look up at it, as the door was immediately opened by an elderly female who was intended to wait upon them.

Soon after they entered the cottage, Jack Pringle and the coachman entered the passage with the small amount of luggage which they had brought with them. This was deposited in the passage, and then Jack went out again and, after a few minutes, there was the sound of wheels which intimated that the coach had driven off.

Jack, however, returned a few minutes afterwards, having secured the wicket-gate at the end of the garden, and then entered the house, shutting the door carefully after him.

Flora and her mother looked over the apartments which they were shown with some surprise. It was everything that they could wish; indeed, though it could not be termed handsomely or extravagantly furnished, or that the things were new, yet there was all that convenience and comfort could require as well as some luxuries.

"Well," said Flora, "this is very thoughtful of the Admiral. The place will really be charming, and the garden too, delightful."

"Mustn't be made use of just now," said Jack, "if you please, ma'am; them's the orders at present."

"Very well," said Flora, smiling. "I suppose, Mr. Pringle, we must obey them."

"Jack Pringle, if you please," said Jack. "My command's only temporary. I ain't got a commission."

The Flight Of The Vampyre

Chapter 57
The Lonely Watch, and the Adventure in the Deserted House

It is now night-time, and a peculiar and solemn stillness reigns in and about Bannerworth Hall and its surrounding grounds; one might have supposed it to be a place of the dead, deserted completely after sunset by all who were living. There was not a breath of air stirring, and this circumstance added greatly to the impression of profound repose which the whole scene exhibited. We may imagine the sort of desolation that reigned through Bannerworth Hall when for the first time after nearly a hundred and fifty years of occupation, it was deserted by the representatives of that family, so many members of which had lived and died beneath its roof. It seemed as if twenty years of continued occupation could not have produced such an effect upon the ancient edifice as had those few hours of neglect and desertion.

And yet it was not as if it had been stripped of those time-worn and ancient relics of ornament and furnishing that so long had furnished it. No, nothing but the absence of those people who had been accustomed quietly to move from room to room deepened its air of dreary repose and listlessness.

The shutters, too, were all closed, and that circumstance contributed largely to the gloominess of the rooms.

In fact, anything which could be done without attracting very special observation was done to prove to any casual observer that the house was untenanted.

But such was not really the case. In that very room where the much dreaded Varney the vampyre had made one of his dreaded appearances to Flora Bannerworth and her mother, sat two men.

They were sitting in silence in the room from which Flora had discharged the pistol which had been left to her by her brother.

It was a room which was very accessible from the gardens, for it had long French windows which opened onto the grounds, and only a stone step intervened between the flooring of the apartment and a broad gravel walk which wound round that entire portion of the house.

Before them on a table were several articles of refreshment, as well of defense and offence, according to need.

There were a bottle and three glasses, and lying near the elbow of one of the men was a large pair of pistols, such as might have adorned the belt of some desperate character who wished to instill an opinion of his prowess into his foes by the magnitude of his weapons.

Close to the same man lay some more modern fire-arms, as well as a long knife which possessed a silver mounted handle.

The only light they had consisted of a large lantern, constructed with a slide, so that it could be completely obscured at a moment's notice, but now as it was placed, the rays that were allowed to come from it were directed as much away from the window of the apartment as possible; they fell upon the faces of the two men, revealing them to be Admiral Bell and Dr. Chillingworth.

It might have been the effect of the particular light in which he sat, but the doctor looked extremely pale and did not appear at all at his ease. The Admiral, on the contrary, appeared in as placid a state of mind as possible, and had his arms folded across his breast, and his head shrunk down between his shoulders, as if he had made up his mind to something that was to last a long time and, therefore, he was making the best of it.

"I do hope," said Mr. Chillingworth, after a long pause, "that our efforts will be crowned with success — you know, my dear sir, that I have always been of your opinion, that there was a great deal more in this matter than met the eye."

"To be sure," said the Admiral, "and as to our efforts being crowned with success, why, I'll give you a toast, doctor, 'may the morning's reflection provide for the evening's amusement.'"

"Ha! Ha!" said Chillingworth faintly; "I'd rather not drink any more, and you seem, Admiral, to have transposed the toast in some way. I believe it runs, 'may the evening's amusement bear the morning's reflection.'"

"Transpose the devil!" said the Admiral; "what do I care how it runs? I gave you my toast; why don't you drink?"

"Why, my dear sir, medically speaking I am strongly of the opinion that when the human stomach is made to contain a large quantity of alcohol, it produces bad effects upon the system. Now, I've certainly taken one glass of this infernally strong Hollands[xv] ale, and it is now lying in my stomach like the red-hot heater of a tea-urn."

"Is it? Put it out with another then," he said affably.

"Ay, I'm afraid that would not answer, but do you really think, Admiral, that we shall effect anything by waiting here, keeping watch and ward, and not under the most comfortable circumstances this first night of the Hall being empty."

"Well, I don't know that we shall," said the Admiral; "but when you really want to steal a march upon the enemy, there is nothing like beginning betimes. We are both of the opinion that Varney's great object throughout has been, by some means or another, to get possession of the house."

"Yes; true, true," agreed Mr. Chillingworth.

"We know that he has been unceasing in his endeavors to get the Bannerworth family out of it; that he has offered them their own price to become its tenant, and that the whole gist of his quiet and placid interview with Flora in the garden was to supply her with a new set of reasons for urging her mother and brothers to leave Bannerworth Hall, because the old ones were certainly not found sufficient."

"True, true, most true," said Mr. Chillingworth, emphatically. "You know, sir, that from the first time you broached that view of the subject to me, how entirely I coincided with you."

"Of course you did, for you are an honest fellow, and a right-thinking fellow, although you are a doctor, and I don't know that I like doctors much better than I like lawyers – they're only humbugs in a different sort of way. But I wish to be liberal; there is such a thing as an honest lawyer and, damne, you're an honest doctor!"

"Of course I'm much obliged, Admiral, for your good opinion. I only wish it had struck me to bring something of a solid nature in the shape of food to sustain myself during the hours we shall have to wait here."

"Don't trouble yourself about that," said the Admiral. "Do you think I'm a donkey and would set out on a cruise without stocking my ship? I should think not. Jack Pringle will be here soon, and he has my orders to bring in something to eat."

"Well," said the doctor, "that's very provident of you, Admiral, and I feel personally obliged, but tell me, how do you intend to conduct the watch?"

"What do you mean?"

"Why, I mean, if we sit here with the window fastened so as to prevent our light from being seen, and the door closed, how are we by any possibility to know if the house is attacked or not?"

"Hark'ee, my friend," said the Admiral; "I've left a weak point for the enemy."

"A what, Admiral?"

"A weak point. I've taken good care to secure everything but one of the windows on the ground floor, and I've left that open, or so nearly open that it will look like the most natural place in the world to get in at. Now, just inside that window, I've placed a lot of the family crockery. I'll warrant, if anybody so much as puts his foot in, you'll hear the smash; – and, damne, there it is!"

There was a long crash at this moment, followed by a succession of similar sounds, but of a lesser degree, and both the Admiral and Mr. Chillingworth sprung to their feet.

"Come on," cried the former; "here'll be a precious row – take the lantern."

Mr. Chillingworth did so, but he did not seem possessed of a great deal of presence of mind, for, before they got out of the room, he twice accidentally put on the dark slide and produced a total darkness.

"Damn!" blustered the Admiral; "don't make it wink and wink in that way; hold it up, and run after me as hard as you can."

"I'm coming, I'm coming," said Mr. Chillingworth.

It was one of the windows of a long room, containing five, fronting the garden, which the Admiral had left purposely unguarded, and it was not far from the apartment in which they had been sitting, so that not a half a minute's time elapsed between the moment of the first alarm and their reaching the spot from whence it was presumed to arise.

The Admiral had armed himself with one of the huge pistols, and he dashed forward towards the window where he knew he had placed the family crockery, and where he fully expected to meet the reward of his exertion by discovering someone lying amid its fragments.

In this, however, he was disappointed, for although there was evidently a great smash amongst the plates and dishes, the window remained closed, and there was no indication whatever of the presence of any one.

"Well, that's odd," said the Admiral; "I balanced them up amazingly careful, and two of 'em edgeways – damne, a fly would have knocked them down."

"Mew," said a great cat, emerging from under a chair.

"Curse you, there you are," said the Admiral, "Put out the light, put out the light; here we're illuminating the whole house for nothing."

With a click went the darkening slide over the lantern and all was obscurity.

At that instant a shrill, clear whistle came from the garden.

Chapter 58
The Arrival of Jack Pringle – Midnight and the Vampyre – The Mysterious Hat

"Bless me! what is that?" said Mr. Chillingworth; "what a very singular sound."

"Hold your noise," said the Admiral; "did you never hear that before?"

"No; how should I?"

"Lord, bless the ignorance of some people, that's a boatswain's[xvi] call."

"Oh, it is," said Mr. Chillingworth; "is he going to call again?"

"Damne, I tell ye it's a boatswain's call."

"Well then, damne, if it comes to that," said Mr. Chillingworth, "what does he call here for?"

The Admiral disdained an answer, but demanding the lantern, he opened it, so that there was sufficient glimmering of light to guide him, and then walked from the room towards the front door of the Hall.

He asked no questions before he opened it, because no doubt the signal was prearranged, and Jack Pringle, for it was indeed he who had arrived, at once walked in, and the Admiral barred the door with the same precision with which it was before secured.

"Well, Jack," he said, "did you see anybody?"

"Ay, ay, sir," said Jack.

"Why, ye don't mean that – where?"

"Where I bought the grub; a woman ..."

"Damne, you're a fool, Jack."

"You're another."

"Hilloa, ye scoundrel, what d'ye mean by talking to me in that way? Is this your respect for your superiors?"

"Ship's been paid off, long ago," said Jack, "and I ain't got no superiors. I ain't a marine or a Frenchman."

"Why, you're drunk."

"I know it; put that in your eye."

"There's a scoundrel. Why, you know-nothing-lubber, didn't I tell you to be careful, and that everything depended upon secrecy and caution? And didn't I tell you, above all this, to avoid drink?"

"To be sure you did."

"And yet you come here like a rum cask."

"Yes; now you've had your say, what then?"

"You'd better leave him alone," said Mr. Chillingworth; "it's no use arguing with a drunken man."

"Harkye, Admiral," said Jack, steadying himself as well as he could. "I've put up with you a precious long while, but I won't no longer; you're so drunk, now, that you keeping bobbing up and down like the mizzen gaff in a storm – that's my opinion – tol de rol."

"Let him alone, let him alone," urged Mr. Chillingworth. "The villain," said the Admiral; "he's enough to ruin everything; now, who would have thought that? But it's always been the way with him for a matter of twenty years – he never had any judgment in his drink. When it was all smooth sailing, and nothing to do, and the fellow might have got an extra drop on board which nobody would have cared for, he's as sober as a judge but, whenever there's anything to do that wants a little cleverness, confound him, he ships rum enough to float a seventy-four."

"Are you going to stand anything to drink," said Jack, "my old buffer? Do you recollect where you got your knob scuttled off Beirut – how you fell on your latter end and tried to recollect your church catechism, you old brute? – I's ashamed of you. Do you recollect the brown girl you bought for thirteen bob and a tanner at the blessed Society Islands, and sold her again for a dollar to a nigger seven-feet two in his natural pumps? You're a nice article, you is, to talk of marines and swabs, and shore-going lubbers, blow yer. Do you recollect the little Frenchman that told ye he'd pull your blessed nose, and I advised you to soap it?"

"Death and the devil!" said the Admiral, breaking from the grasp of Mr. Chillingworth.

"Ay," said Jack, "you'll come to 'em both one of these days, old cock, and no mistake."

"I'll have his life, I'll have his life," roared the Admiral.

"Nay, nay, sir," said Mr. Chillingworth, catching the Admiral round the waist. "My dear sir, recollect now if I may venture to advise you, Admiral Bell, there's a lot of that fiery Holland's[xvii] you know, in the next room; set him down to that, and finish him off. I'll warrant him, he'll be quiet enough."

"What's that you say?" cried Jack – "Holland's! – Who's got any? – next to rum and Elizabeth Baker, if I has an affection, it's Holland's."

"Jack!" ordered the Admiral.

"Ay, ay, sir!" said Jack, instinctively.

"Come this way."

Jack staggered after him, and they all reached the room where the Admiral and Mr. Chillingworth had been sitting before the alarm.

"There!" said the Admiral, putting the light upon the table and pointing to the bottle; "what do you think of that?"

"I never thinks under such circumstances," said Jack. "Here's to the wooden walls of old England!"

He seized the bottle and, putting its neck into his mouth for a few moments nothing was heard but a gurgling sound of the liquor passing down his throat; his head went further and further back, until, at last, over he went, chair and bottle and all, and lay in a helpless state of intoxication on the floor.

"So far, so good," said the Admiral. "He's out of the way, at all events."

"I'll just loosen his neck-cloth," said Mr. Chillingworth, "and then we'll go and sit somewhere else, and I should recommend that we take up our station in that chamber, once Flora's, where the mysterious paneled portrait hangs that bears such a strong resemblance to Varney, the vampyre."

"Hush!" said the Admiral. "What's that?"

They listened for a moment intently, and then they heard a distinct footstep upon the gravel path outside the window as if some person were walking along, not altogether heedlessly, but yet without any very great amount of caution or attention to the noise he might make.

"Hist!" said the doctor. "Not a word. They come."

"What do you say they for?" said the Admiral.

"Because something seems to whisper me that Mr. Marchdale knows more of Varney the vampyre than ever he has chosen to reveal. Put out the light."

"Yes, yes – that'll do. The moon has risen; see how it streams through the chinks of the shutters."

"No, no – it's not in that direction or our light would have betrayed us. Do you not see the beams come from that half glass-door leading to the greenhouse?"

"Yes, and there's the footstep again, or another."

Tramp, tramp came a footfall upon the gravel path and, as before it died away upon their listening ears.

"What do you say now," said Mr. Chillingworth – "are there not two?"

"If they were a dozen," said the Admiral, "although we have lost one of our force, I would tackle them. Let's creep on through the rooms in the direction the footsteps went."

"My life on it," said Mr. Chillingworth, as they left the apartment, "if this be Varney he makes for that apartment where Flora slept, and which he knows how to get admission to. I've studied the house well, Admiral, and to get to that window anyone from outside must take a considerable round. Come on – we shall be beforehand."

"A good idea – a good idea," the Admiral agreed. "Be it so."

They allowed themselves just barely sufficient light to guide them on the way, and they hurried on with as much precipitation as the intricacies of the passage would allow, nor did they halt until they had reached the chamber where the portrait hung which bore such a striking and remarkable a likeness to Varney, the vampyre.

They left the lamp outside the door so that not even a straggling beam from it could betray that there were persons on the watch, and then, as quietly as foot could fall, they took up their station among the hangings of the antique bedstead.

"Do you think," said the Admiral, "we've beaten them?"

"Certainly we have. It's unlucky that the blind of the window is down."

"Is it? By Heaven, there's a damned strange-looking shadow creeping over it."

Mr. Chillingworth looked with suspended breath. Even he could not altogether get rid of a tremulous feeling as he saw that the shadow of a human form, apparently of very large dimensions, was on the outside with the arms spread out as if feeling for some means of opening the window.

It would have been easy now to fire one of the pistols directly at the figure but, somehow or another, both the Admiral and Mr. Chillingworth shrank from that course, and they felt inclined to capture whoever might make his appearance using their pistols as a last resort.

"Who should you say that was?" whispered the Admiral.

"Varney, the vampyre."

"Damne, he's ill-looking and big enough for anything – there's a noise!"

There was a strange cracking sound at the window as if a pane of glass was being very stealthily and quietly broken, and then the blind was agitated slightly, as if the hand of some person was introduced for the purpose of allowing entrance into the apartment.

"He's coming in," whispered the Admiral.

"Hush, for Heaven's sake!" said Mr. Chillingworth; "you will alarm him, and we shall lose the fruit of all the labor we have already bestowed upon the matter, but did you not say something, Admiral, about lying under the window and catching him by the leg?"

"Why, yes; I did."

"Go and do it, then, for as sure as you are a living man, his leg will be within the room in a minute."

"Here goes," said the Admiral; "I never suggest anything which I'm unwilling to do myself."

Whoever it was that was now making such strenuous exertions to get into the apartment seemed to find some difficulty regarding the fastenings of the window, and as this difficulty increased, the patience of the party deserted him, and the casement was rattled with violence.

With a far greater amount of caution than anyone from a knowledge of his character would have given him credit for, the Admiral crept forward and laid himself exactly under the window.

The depth of the wood-work from the floor to the lowest part of the window-frame did not exceed above two feet; so that anyone could conveniently step in from the balcony outside on to the floor of the apartment, which was just what he who was attempting to gain an entrance was desirous of doing.

It was quite clear that, be he who he might, mortal or vampyre, he had some acquaintance with the fastening of the window, for now he succeeded in moving it, and the sash was thrown open.

The blind was still an obstacle, but a vigorous pull from the intruder brought that down on the prostate Admiral, and then Mr. Chillingworth saw, by the moonlight, a tall, gaunt figure standing in the balcony as if just hesitating for a moment whether to get head first or feet first into the apartment.

Had he chosen the former alternative he would need, indeed, to have been endowed with more than mortal powers of defense to escape capture, but his lucky star was in the ascendancy and he put his foot in first.

He turned his side to the apartment, and as he did so the bright moonlight fell upon his face, enabling Mr. Chillingworth to see without the shadow of a doubt that it was indeed Varney, the vampyre, who was thus stealthily making his entrance into Bannerworth Hall. The doctor scarcely knew whether to be pleased or not at this discovery; it was an almost terrifying one, skeptical as he was upon the subject of vampyres, and he waited breathless for the continuation of the singular and perilous adventure.

No doubt Admiral Bell deeply congratulated himself upon the success which was about to crown his stratagem for the capture of the intruder, no matter whom he might be, and he writhed with impatience for the foot to come sufficiently near him to enable him to grasp it.

His patience was not severely tried, for in another moment it rested upon his chest.

"Boarders ahoy!" shouted the Admiral, and at once he laid hold of the trespasser. "Yard-arm to yard-arm. I think I've got you now. Here's a prize, doctor! He shall go away without his leg if he goes away now. Eh! What! The light – damne, he has – Doctor, the light! the light! Why what' this! – Hilloa, there!"

Dr. Chillingworth sprang into the passage, and procured the light – in another moment he was at the side of the Admiral, and the lantern slide being thrown back, he saw at once the dilemma into which his friend had fallen.

There he lay upon his back, grasping, with the vehemence of an embrace that had in it much of the ludicrous, a long boot from which the intruder had cleverly slipped his leg, leaving it as a poor trophy in the hands of his enemies.

"Why you've only pulled his boot off," said the doctor; "and now he's gone for good for he knows what we're about, and has slipped through your fingers."

Admiral Bell sat up and looked at the boot with a rueful countenance.

"Done again!" he said.

"Yes, you are done," said the doctor; "why didn't you lay hold of the leg while you were about it, instead of the boot? Admiral, are these your tactics?"

"Don't be a fool," said the Admiral; "put out the light and give me the pistols, or blaze away yourself into the garden; a chance shot may do something. It's no use running after him; a stern chase is a long chase, but fire away."

As if some parties below had heard him give his word, two loud reports from the garden immediately ensued, and a crash of glass testified to the fact that some deadly missile had entered the room.

"Murder!" said the doctor, falling flat upon his back. "I don't like this at all; it's all in your line, Admiral, but not in mine."

"All's right, my lad," said the Admiral; "now for it."

He saw laying in the moonlight the pistols which he and the doctor had brought into the room, and in another moment he returned the broadside of the enemy.

"Damn it!" he roared; "This puts me in mind of old times. Blaze away, you thieves, while I load; broadside to broadside. It's your turn now; I scorn to take an advantage. What the devil's that?"

Something very large and very heavy came bang against the window, sending it all into the room, and nearly smothering the Admiral with the fragments. Another shot was then fired, and in came something else which hit the wall on the opposite side of the room, rebounding from thence onto the doctor, who gave a yell of despair.

After that all was still; the enemy seemed to be satisfied that he had silenced the garrison. And it took the Admiral a great deal of kicking and plunging to rescue himself from some mass that was upon him, which seemed to him to be a considerable sized tree.

"Call this fair fighting," he shouted, "getting a man's legs and arms tangled up like a piece of Indian matting in the branches of a tree? Doctor, I say! Hilloa! Where are you?"

"I don't know," said the doctor; "but there's somebody getting into the balcony – now we shall be murdered in cold blood."

"Where's the pistols?"

"Fired off, of course; you did it yourself."

Bang came something else into the room, which, from the sound it made, closely resembled a brick, and after that somebody jumped clean into the centre of the floor, and then, after rolling and writhing about in a most singular manner, slowly got up, and, with various preliminary hiccups, said, "Come on, you lubbers, many of you as like. I'm the tar for all weathers."

"Why, damne," said the Admiral, "it's Jack Pringle."

"Yes it is," slurred Jack, who was not sufficiently sober to recognize the Admiral's voice. "I sees as how you've heard of me. Come on, all of you."

"Why, Jack, you scoundrel," roared the Admiral, "how came you here? Don't you know me? I'm your Admiral, you horse-marine."

"Eh?" said Jack. "Ay – ay, sir, how came you here?"

"How came you, you villain?"

"Boarded the enemy."

"The enemy who you boarded was us, and hang me if I don't think you haven't been pouring broadsides into us, while the enemy were running before the wind in another direction."

"Lord!" said Jack.

"Explain, you scoundrel, explain."

"Well, that's only reasonable," said Jack, and giving a heavier lurch than usual, he sat down with a great bounce upon the floor. "You see it's just this here, – when I was a coming of course I heard, just as I was a going, that ere as made me come all in consequence of somebody a going, or for to come, you see, Admiral."

"Doctor," cried the Admiral in a great rage, "just help me out of this entanglement of branches, and I'll rid the world from an encumbrance by smashing that fellow."

"Smash yourself!" said Jack. "You know you're drunk."

"My dear Admiral," Mr. Chillingworth said, laying hold of one of his legs and pulling it very hard, which brought his face into a lot of brambles, "we're making a mess of this business."

"Murder!" shouted the Admiral; "you are indeed. Is that what you call pulling me out of it? You've stuck me fast."

"I'll manage it," said Jack. "I've seed him in many a scrape, and I've seed him out. You pull me, doctor, and I'll pull him. Yo hoy!"
Jack laid hold of the Admiral by the scuff of the neck, and the doctor laid hold of Jack round the waist, and consequently he was dragged out from under the branches of the tree which seemed to have been thrown into the room. And down fell both Jack and the doctor. At this instant there was a strange hissing sound heard below the window; then there was a sudden loud report, as if a hand-grenade had gone off.

A spectral sort of light gleamed into the room, and a tall, gaunt-looking figure rose slowly up in the balcony.

"Beware of the dead!" said a voice. "Let the living contend with the living, the dead with the dead. Beware!"

The figure disappeared, as did also the strange, spectral-looking light. A deathlike silence ensued, and the cold moonbeams streamed in upon the floor of the apartment as if nothing had occurred to disturb the serenity of the scene.

Chapter 59
The Warning – The New Plot of Operation – The Insulting Message from Varney

So much of the night had been consumed in these operations that even had the three personages who lay upon floor of what might be called the haunted chamber of Bannerworth Hall been disposed to seek repose, they would have had a short time to do so before the daylight would stream in upon them, and rouse them to the bustle of waking existence.

It may be well believed what a vast amount of surprise came over the three persons in that chamber at the last little circumstance that had occurred.

There was nothing which had preceded it, that had not resemble a genuine human attack upon the premises, but about that last mysterious appearance with its curious light there was quite enough to bother the Admiral and Jack Pringle to a considerable degree, whatever might be the effect upon Mr. Chillingworth whose profession better enabled him to comprehend, chemically, what would produce such effects.

What with his intoxication and the violent exercise he had taken, Jack was again thoroughly prostrate; while the Admiral could not have looked more astonished had the evil one himself appeared in person and given him notice to quit the premises.

He was, however, the first to speak, and the words he spoke were addressed to Jack, to whom he said, "Jack, you lubber, what do you think of all that?"

The Flight Of The Vampyre

Jack was too far gone even to say "Ay, ay, sir;" and Mr. Chillingworth, slowly getting himself up to his feet, approached the Admiral.

"It's hard to say so much, Admiral Bell," he said, "but it strikes me that whatever object this Sir Francis Varney, or Varney, the vampyre, has in coming into Bannerworth Hall, it is of sufficient importance to induce him to go to great lengths, and not to let even a life stand in the way of its accomplishment."

"Well, it seems so," agreed the Admiral; "for I'll be hanged if I can make head or tail of the fellow."

"If we value our personal safety," Mr. Chillingworth began, "we shall hesitate to continue a perilous adventure which I think can end only in defeat, if not in death."

"But we don't value our personal safety," said the Admiral, "we've got into the adventure, and I don't see why we shouldn't carry it out. It may be growing a little serious, but what of that? For the sake of that young girl, Flora Bannerworth, as well as for the sake of my nephew, Charles Holland, I will see the end of this affair; let it be what it may, but mind you Mr. Chillingworth, if one man chooses to go upon a desperate service, that's no reason why he should ask another to do so."

"I understand you," said Mr. Chillingworth; "but, having commenced the adventure with you, I am not the man to desert you in it. We have committed a great mistake."

"A mistake! How?"

"Why, we ought to have watched outside the house instead of within it. There can be no doubt that if we had lain in wait in the garden, we should have been in a better position to have accomplished our object."

"Well, I don't know, doctor, but it seems to me that if Jack Pringle hadn't made such a fool of himself, we should have managed very well, and I don't know how he came to behave in the manner he did."

"Nor I," said Mr. Chillingworth. "But, at all events, so far as the results go, it is quite clear that any further watching in this house for the appearance of Sir Francis Varney will now be in vain. He has nothing to do now but to keep quiet until we are tired out, and then he immediately can, without trouble, walk into the premises and do whatever is to his own satisfaction."

"But what the deuce can he want upon the premises?"

"That question, Admiral, induces me to think that we have made another mistake. We ought not to have attempted to surprise Sir Francis Varney in coming into Bannerworth Hall, but to catch him as he came out."

"Well, there's something in that. This is a pretty night's business, to be sure. However, it can't be helped; it's done, and there's an end on it. And now as the morning is near at hand, I certainly must confess I should like to get some breakfast, although I don't like that we should all leave the house together."

"Why, as we have now no secret to keep with regard to our being here because the principal person we wished to keep it from is aware of it, I think we cannot do better than send at once for Henry Bannerworth, tell him of the non-success of the effort we have made in his behalf, and admit him at once into our consultation of what is next to be done."

"Agreed, agreed; I thought that, without troubling him, we might have captured this Varney, but that's over now, and as soon as Jack Pringle chooses to wake up again, I'll send him to the Bannerworths with a message."

"Ay, ay, sir," said Jack, suddenly; "all's right."

"Why, you vagabond," said the Admiral, "I do believe you've been shamming."

"Shamming what?"

"Being drunk, to be sure."

"Lor! I couldn't do it," protested Jack; "I'll just tell you how it was. I wakened up and found myself shut in somewhere, and as I couldn't get out of the door, I thought I'd try the window, and there I did get out. Well, perhaps I wasn't quite the thing, but I sees two people in the garden a looking up at this ere room, and to be sure, I thought it was you and the doctor. Well, it warn't no business of mine to interfere, so I seed one of you climb up the balcony, as I thought, and then come down head over heels with such a run that I thought you must have broken your neck."

"But who threw such a confounded lot of things into the room?"

"Why, I did, of course; I had but one pistol, and when I fired that off, I was forced to make up a broadside with what I could."

"Was there ever such a stupid!" grumbled the Admiral; "doctor, doctor, you talked of us making two mistakes, but you forgot a third and worse one still, and that was the bringing such a lubberly son of a seacook into the place as this fellow."

"You're another," said Jack; "and you knows it."

"Well, well," said Mr. Chillingworth, "it's no use continuing to berate him Admiral; Jack, in his way, did, I dare say, what he considered for the best."

"I wish he'd do what he considers for the worst, next time."

"Perhaps I may," Jack said, "and then you will be served out above a bit. What would become of you, I wonder, if it wasn't for me? I'm as good as a mother to you, you knows that, you old babby."

"Come, come, Admiral," said Mr. Chillingworth; "come down to the garden gate; it is now just upon daybreak, and the probability is that we shall not be long there before we see some of the country people who will get us anything we require in the shape of refreshment, and as for Jack, he seems quite sufficiently recovered now to go to the Bannerworths'."

"Oh! I can go," said Jack; "as for that, the only thing as puts me out of the way is the want of something to drink. My constitution won't stand what they call temperance[xviii] living, or nothing with the chill off."

"Go at once," said the Admiral, "and tell Mr. Henry Bannerworth that we are here, but do not tell him in front of his sister or his mother. If you meet anybody on the road, send them here with a cargo of food. It strikes me that a good, comfortable breakfast wouldn't be at all amiss, doctor."

"How rapidly the day dawns," remarked Mr. Chillingworth walking into the balcony from whence Varney, the vampire, had attempted to make good his entrance to the Hall.

Just as he spoke, and before Jack Pringle could get half way over to the garden gate, there came a tremendous ring at the bell which was suspended over it.

A view of that gate could not be commanded from the window of the haunted apartment, so that they could not see who it was that demanded admission.

As Jack Pringle was going down they saw no necessity for personal interference, and he proved that there was not, by presently returning with a note which he said had been thrown over the gate by a lad, who then scampered off with all the speed he could make.

The note had all the appearance of great care having been bestowed upon its folding and sealing. It was duly addressed to "Admiral Bell,

Bannerworth Hall," and the word "immediate" was written at one corner.

The Admiral, after looking at it for some time with very great wonder, came at last to the conclusion that probably to open it would be the shortest way of arriving at a knowledge of who had sent it, and he accordingly did so.

The note was as follows:

> My dear sir, – Feeling assured that you cannot be surrounded with those means and appliances for comfort in the Hall in its now deserted condition which you have a right to expect, and so eminently deserve, I flatter myself that I shall receive an answer in the affirmative when I request the favor of your company to breakfast, as well as that of your learned friend, Mr. Chillingworth.
>
> In consequence of a little accident which occurred last evening to my own residence, I am, at present, until the county builds it up for me again, staying at a house called Walmesley Lodge, where I shall expect you with all the impatience of one soliciting an honor, and hoping that it will be conferred upon him.
>
> I trust that any little difference of opinion on other subjects will not interfere to prevent the harmony of our morning's meal together.
>
> Believe me to be, my dear sir, with the greatest possible consideration, your very obedient, humble servant, 'FRANCIS VARNEY.'

The Admiral gasped again, and looked at Mr. Chillingworth, and then at the note, and then at Mr. Chillingworth again, as if he was perfectly bewildered.

"That's about the coolest piece of business," said Mr. Chillingworth, "that ever I heard of."

"Hang me," the Admiral agreed, "if I sha'n't like the fellow at last. It is cool, and I like it because it is cool. Where's my hat? Where's my stick?"

"What are you going to do?"

"Accept his invitation; to be sure, and breakfast with him and my learned friend as he calls you, I hope you'll come likewise. I'll take the fellow at his word. By fair means, or by foul, I'll know what he wants here, and why he persecutes this family for whom I have an attachment, and what hand he has in the disappearance of my nephew, Charles Holland, for, as sure as there's a Heaven above us, he's at the bottom of that affair. Where is this Walmesley Lodge?"

"Close by in the neighborhood, but... "

"Come on, then; come on."

"But, really, Admiral, you don't mean to say you'll breakfast with – with..."

"A vampyre? Yes, I would, and will, and mean to do so. Here, Jack, you needn't go to Mr. Bannerworth's yet. Come, my learned friend, let's take Time by the forelock."

Chapter 60
The Interrupted Breakfast at Sir Francis Varney's

Despite all Mr. Chillingworth could say to the contrary, the Admiral really meant to breakfast with Sir Francis Varney. The worthy doctor believed for some time that the Admiral must be joking when he talked in such a strain, but he was very soon convinced to the contrary because the latter actually walked out and once more asked him, Mr. Chillingworth, if he meant to go with him, or not.

This was conclusive, so the doctor said, "Well, Admiral, this appears to me rather a mad sort of freak, but as I have begun the adventure with you, I will conclude it with you."

"That's right," said the Admiral; "I'm not deceived in you, doctor; so come along. Hang these vampyres, I don't know how to tackle them myself. I think, after all, Sir Francis Varney is more in your line than he is in mine."

"How do you mean?"

"Why, couldn't you persuade him he's ill and wants some physic? That would soon settle him, you know."

"Settle him!" exclaimed Mr. Chillingworth; "I beg to say that if I did give him any physic, the dose would be much to his advantage, but my opinion is that this invitation to breakfast is a mere piece of irony, and that when we get to Walmesley Lodge, we shall not see anything of him; on the contrary, we shall probably find it's a hoax."

The Flight Of The Vampyre

"I certainly should like that, but still it's worth the trying. The fellow has really behaved himself in such an extraordinary manner that if I can make terms with him, I will, and there's one thing you know, doctor, that I think we may say we have discovered."

"And what may that be? Is it not to make too sure of a vampyre, even when you have him by the leg?"

"No, that ain't it, though that's a very good thing in its way, but it is just this, that Sir Francis Varney, whoever he is and whatever he is, is after Bannerworth Hall and not the Bannerworth family. If you recollect, Mr. Chillingworth, in all of our conversations I have always insisted upon that fact."

"You have, and it seems to me to be completely verified by the proceedings of the night. Admiral, there is the great mystery — what can he want at Bannerworth Hall that makes him take such a world of trouble and run so many fearful risks in trying to get at it?"

"That is, indeed, the mystery, and if he really means this invitation to breakfast, I shall ask him plainly, and tell him at the same time, that possibly his very best way to secure his object will be to be candid, vampyre as he is."

"But really, Admiral, you do not still cling to that foolish superstition of believing that Sir Francis Varney is in reality a vampyre?"

"I don't know, and I can't say; if anybody was to give me a description of a strange sort of fish that I had never seen, I wouldn't take upon myself to say there ain't such a thing, nor would you, doctor, if you had really seen the many odd ones that I have encountered at various times."

"Well, well, Admiral, I'm certainly not belonging to that school of philosophy which declares the impossible to be what it don't understand; there may be vampyres, and there may be apparitions for all I know to the contrary; I only doubt these things because I think, if they were true, that as a phenomena of nature they would have been by this time established by repeated instances without the possibility of doubt or debate."

Well, there's something in that, but how far have we got to go now?"

"No further than to yonder enclosure where you see those park-like looking gates and that cedar-tree stretching its dark-green foliage so far into the road; this is Walmesley Lodge, where you have been invited."

The Flight Of The Vampyre

"And you, my learned friend, recollect that you were invited too; so that you are no intruder upon the hospitality of Varney, the vampyre."

"I say, Admiral," said Mr. Chillingworth, when they reached the gates, "you know it is not quite the thing to call a man a vampyre at his own breakfast-table, so just oblige me by promising not to make any such remark to Sir Francis."

"A likely thing!" said the Admiral; "he knows I know what he is, and he knows I'm a plain man and a blunt speaker; however, I'll be civil to him, and more than that I can't promise. I must wring out of him, if I can, what has become of Charles Holland and what the deuce he really wants himself."

"Well, well; come to no collision with him while we're his guests."

"Not if I can help it."

The doctor rang the gate bell of Walmesley Lodge, and was in a few moments answered by a woman demanding their business.

"Is Sir Francis Varney here?" asked the doctor.

"Oh, ah! yes," she replied; "you see his house was burnt down for something or other – I'm sure I don't know what – by some people – I'm sure I don't know who; so as the lodge was to let, we have took him in till he can suit himself."

"Ah! That's it, is it?" said the Admiral; "tell him that Admiral Bell and Dr. Chillingworth are here."

"Very well," said the woman; "you may walk in."

"Thank you; you're vastly obliging, ma'am. Is there anything going on in the breakfast line?"

"Well, yes; I am getting him some breakfast, but he didn't say as he expected company."

The woman opened the garden gate, and they walked up a trimly laid out garden to the lodge, which was a cottage-like structure in external appearance, although inside it boasted of all the comforts of a tolerably extensive house.

She left them in a small room off the hall, and was absent about five minutes; when she returned she merely said that Sir Francis Varney presented his compliments, and desired them to walk upstairs. She preceded them up a handsome flight which led to the first floor of the lodge.

Up to this moment Mr. Chillingworth had expected some excuses for, notwithstanding all he had heard and seen of Sir Francis Varney, he could not believe that any amount of impudence would suffice to

The Flight Of The Vampyre

enable him to receive people as his guests with whom he must feel that he was at such positive war.

It was a singular circumstance, and perhaps the only thing that matched the cool impertinence of the invitation, was the acceptance of it under the circumstances by the Admiral.

Sir Francis Varney might have intended it as a jest, but if he did, so it was evident he would not allow himself to be beaten with his own weapons.

The room into which they were shown was a longish narrow one; a very wide door gave them admission to it, at the end nearest the staircase, and at its other extremity there was a similar door opening into some other apartments of the house.

Sir Francis Varney sat with his back towards this second door, and a table with some chairs and other articles of furniture were so arranged before him that while they seemed to be carelessly placed in the position they occupied, they really formed a pretty good barrier between him and his visitors.

The Admiral, however, was too intent upon getting a sight of Varney to notice any preparation of this sort, and he advanced quickly into the room.

And there, indeed, was the much dreaded, troublesome, persevering, and singular looking being who had caused such a world of annoyance to the family of the Bannerworths, as well as disturbing the peace of the whole district which had the misfortune to have him as an inhabitant.

If anything, he looked thinner, taller, and paler than usual, and there seemed to be a slight nervousness of manner about him as he slowly inclined his head towards the Admiral, which was a new manifestation for Varney, the vampyre.

"Well," said Admiral Bell, "you invited me to breakfast, me and my learned friend; here we are."

"No two human beings," Varney said, "could be more welcome to my hospitality than yourself and Dr. Chillingworth. I pray you to be seated. What a pleasant thing it is, after the toils and struggles of this life, occasionally to sit down in the sweet companionship of such dear friends." He made a hideous face as he spoke, and the Admiral looked as if he were half inclined to quarrel at that early stage of the proceedings.

"Dear friends!" he expostulated; "well, well – it's no use squabbling about a word or two, but I tell you what it is, Mr. Varney, or Sir Francis Varney, or whatever your name is… "

"Hold, my dear sir," said Varney, "after breakfast, if you please – after breakfast."

He rang a hand-bell as he spoke, and the woman who had charge of the house brought in a tray tolerably covered with the materials for a substantial morning's meal. She placed it upon the table, and certainly the various articles that smoked upon it did great credit to her culinary powers.

"Deborah," said Sir Varney in a mild sort of tone, "keep on bringing things to eat until this old brutal sea-ruffian has satiated his disgusting appetite."

The Admiral opened his eyes an enormous width and, looking at Sir Francis Varney, he placed his two fists upon the table and drew a long breath.

"Did you address those observations to me," he said at length, "you blood-sucking vagabond?"

"Eh?" said Sir Francis Varney, looking over the Admiral's head as if he saw something interesting on the wall beyond.

"My dear Admiral," said Mr. Chillingworth, "Come away."

"I'll see you damned first! Now, Mr. Vampyre, no shuffling; did you address those observations to me?"

"Deborah," murmured Sir Francis Varney in silvery tones, "you can remove this tray and bring on the next."

"Not if I know it," said the Admiral. "I came to breakfast, and I'll have it; after breakfast I'll pull your nose – ay, if you were fifty vampyres, I'd do it."

"Dr. Chillingworth," said Varney, without paying the least attention to what the Admiral said, "you don't eat, my dear sir; you must be fatigued with your night's exertions. A man of your age, you know, cannot be supposed to roll and tumble about like a fool in a pantomime with impunity. Only think what a calamity it would be if you were laid up. Your patients would all get well, you know."

"Sir Francis Varney," said Mr. Chillingworth, "we're your guests; we came here at your invitation to partake of a meal. You have wantonly attacked both of our characters. I need not say that by so doing you cast a far greater slur upon your own taste and judgment than you can upon us."

The Flight Of The Vampyre

"Admirably spoken," said Sir Francis Varney, giving his hands a clap together that made the Admiral jump again. "Now, old Bell, I'll fight you, if you think yourself aggrieved, while the doctor sees fair play."

"Old who?" shouted the Admiral.

"Bell, Bell – is not your name Bell? – a family name, I presume, on account of the infernal clack, clack, without any sense in it, that is characteristic of your race."

"You'll fight me?" said the Admiral, jumping up.

"Yes, if you challenge me."

"By Jove I do; of course."

"Then I accept it, and the challenged party, you know well, or ought to know, can make his own terms in the encounter."

"Make what terms you please; I care not what they are. Only say you will fight, and that's sufficient."

"It is well," said Sir Francis Varney, in a solemn tone.

"Nay, nay," interrupted Mr. Chillingworth; "this is boyish folly."

"Hold your row," the Admiral told him, "and let's hear what he's got to say."

"In this mansion," said Sir Francis Varney – "for a mansion it is although under the unpretending name of a lodge – in this mansion there is a large apartment which was originally fitted up by a scientific proprietor of the place for the purpose of microscopic and other experiments which required a darkness total and complete, such a darkness as seems as if it could be felt – palpable, thick, and obscure as the darkness of the tomb, and I know what that is."

"The devil you do!" said the Admiral. "It's damp, too, ain't it?"

"The room?"

"No; the grave."

"Oh! uncommonly damp after autumnal rains. But to resume – this room is large, lofty, and perfectly empty."

"Well?"

"I propose that we procure two scythes."

"Two what?"

"Scythes, with their long handles, their convenient holding places, and their sharp curved blades."

"Well, I'll be hanged! What do you propose next?"

"You may be hanged. The next is that with these scythes we be both of us placed in the darkened room and the door closed and doubly locked upon us for one hour, and that then and there we do our best to cut each other in two. If you succeed in dismembering me, you will have won the day, but I hope, from my superior agility" – here Sir Francis jumped upon his chair, and sat upon the back of it – "to get the better of you. How do you like the plan I have proposed? Does it meet your wishes?"

"Curse your impudence!" said the Admiral, placing his elbows upon the table, and resting his chin in astonishment upon his two hands.

"Nay," interrupted Sir Francis, "you challenged me, and besides, you'll have an equal chance, you know that. If you succeed in striking me first, down I go; whereas, if I succeed in striking you first, down you go."

As he spoke, Sir Francis Varney stretched out his foot and closed a small bracket which held out the flap of the table on which the Admiral was leaning and, accordingly, down the Admiral went, tea-tray and all.

Mr. Chillingworth ran to help him up, and, when they both recovered their feet, they found they were alone.

Chapter 61
The Mysterious Stranger – The Particulars of the Suicide at Bannerworth Hall

"Where the hell is he?" roared the Admiral. "Was there ever such a confounded take-in?"

"Well, I really don't know," Mr. Chillingworth replied; "but it seems to me that he must have gone out of that door that was behind him. I begin, do you know, Admiral, to wish..."

"What?"

"That we had never come here at all, and I think that the sooner we get out of it, the better."

"Yes, but I am not going to be hoaxed and humbugged in this way. I will have satisfaction, but not with those confounded scythes and things he talks about in the dark room. Give me broad daylight and no favor; yardarm and yardarm; broadside and broadside; hand-grenades and marling-spikes."

"Well, but that's what he won't do. Now, Admiral, listen to me."

"Well, go on; what next?"

"Come away at once."

"Oh, you said that before."

"Yes, but I'm going to say something else. Look round you. Don't you think this is a large, scientific-looking room?"

"What of that?"

"Why, what if it was to become as dark as the grave, and Varney was to enter with his scythe, that he talks of, and begin mowing about our legs."

"The devil! Come along!"

The door at which they entered was at this moment opened, and the old woman made her appearance.

"Please, sir," she said, "here's a Mr. Mortimer," in a loud voice. "Oh, Sir Francis ain't here! Where's he gone, gentlemen?"

"To the devil! Who may Mr. Mortimer be?"

There walked past the woman a stout, portly-looking man, well dressed, but with a very odd look upon his face, in consequence of crossed eyes which prevented quite seeing which way he was looking.

"I must see him," he said in a surprisingly weedy tone; "I must see him."

Mr. Chillingworth started back as if in amazement.

"Good God!" he cried, "you here?"

"Confusion!" stammered Mr. Mortimer; "are you Dr. – Dr...."

"Chillingworth."

"The same. Hush! There is no occasion to betray – that is, to state my secret."

"And mine, too," averred Mr. Chillingworth. "But what brings you here?"

"I cannot and dare not tell you. Farewell!"

He turned abruptly, and was leaving the room but he ran against someone at the entrance, and in another moment Henry Bannerworth, heated and almost breathless by evident haste, made his appearance.

"Hilloa! Bravo!" cried the Admiral; "the more the merrier! Here's a combined squadron! Why, how came you here, Mr. Henry Bannerworth?"

"Bannerworth!" Mortimer; exclaimed, "is this young man's name Bannerworth?"

"Yes," Henry answered. "Do you know me, sir?"

"No, no; only I – I – must be off. Does anyone know anything of Sir Francis Varney?"

"We did know something of him," replied the Admiral, "a little while ago, but he's taken himself off. Don't you do likewise. If you've got anything to say, stop and say it like an Englishman."

"Stuff! Stuff!" responded Mr. Mortimer impatiently. "What do you all want here?"

"Why, Sir Francis Varney," said Henry, "and I care not if the whole world heard it – is the persecutor of my family."

"How? In what way?"

"He has the reputation of a vampyre; he has hunted me and mine from house and home."

"Indeed!"

"Yes," cried Dr. Chillingworth; "by some means or another, he seems determined to get possession of Bannerworth Hall."

"Well, gentlemen," said Mortimer, "I promise you that I will inquire into this. Mr. Chillingworth, I did not expect to meet you. Perhaps the least we say to each other is, after all, the better."

"Let me ask but one question," implored Dr. Chillingworth.

"Ask it."

"Did he live after…?"

"Hush! He did."

"You always told me to the contrary."

"Yes; I had an object; the game is up. Farewell, and, gentlemen, as I am making my exit, let me do so with a sentiment: – Society at large is divided into two great classes."

"And what may they be?" said the Admiral.

"Those who have been hanged, and those who have not. Adieu!" He turned and left the room, and Mr. Chillingworth sank into a chair, and said in a low voice, "It is uncommonly true, and I've found out an acquaintance among the former."

"Damn it! You seem all mad! I can't make out what you are about. How came you to be here, Mr. Henry Bannerworth?"

"By mere accident, I heard that you were keeping watch and ward in the Hall. Admiral, it was cruel and not well done of you to attempt such an enterprise without acquainting me with it. Did you suppose for a moment that I, who had the greatest interest in this affair, would have shrunk from danger, if danger there be, or lacked perseverance if that quality were necessary in carrying out any plan by which the safety and honor of my family might be preserved?"

"Nay, now, my young friend," interrupted Mr. Chillingworth.

"Nay, sir, but I take it ill that I should have been kept out of this affair, and it should have been sedulously, as it were, kept a secret from me."

"Let him go on as he likes," said the Admiral; "boys will be boys. After all, you know, doctor, it's my affair and not yours. Let him say what he likes; where's the odds? It's of no consequence."

"I do not expect, Admiral Bell," said Henry, "that it is of the same consequence to you as it is to me."

"Psha!"

"Respecting you, sir, as I do…"

"Gammon[xix]!"

"I must confess that I did expect…"

"What you didn't get; therefore, there's an end of that. Now, I tell you what, Henry, Sir Francis Varney is within this house; at least I have reason to suppose so."

"Then," exclaimed Henry, impetuously, "I will wring from him answers to various questions which concern my peace and happiness."

"Please, gentlemen," said the woman Deborah, making her appearance, "Sir Francis Varney has gone out, and he says I'm to show all you gentlemen the door as soon as it is convenient for you all to walk out of it."

"I feel convinced," Mr. Chillingworth said, "that it will now be a useless search to attempt to find Sir Francis Varney here. Let me beg of you all to come away, and believe me that I do not speak lightly or with a view to get you away from here when I say that after I have heard something from you, Henry, which I shall ask you to relate to me, painful though it may be, I shall be able to suggest some explanation of many things which appear at present obscure, and to put you in a course of freeing yourself from difficulties which surround you, which, Heaven knows, I little expected I should have it in my power to propose to any of you."

"I will follow your advice, Mr. Chillingworth," agreed Henry; "for I have always found that it has been dictated by good feeling as well as correct judgment. Admiral Bell, you will oblige me much by coming away with me now and at once."

"Well," remarked the Admiral, "if the doctor has really something to say, it alters the appearance of things, and of course I have no objection to coming with you."

Upon this, the whole three of them immediately left the place, and it was evident that Mr. Chillingworth had something of an uncomfortable character upon his mind. He was unusually silent and reserved, and when he did speak, he seemed rather inclined to turn the conversation upon indifferent topics than to add anything more to what he had said upon the deeply interesting one which held so foremost a place in all their minds.

"How is Flora, now," he asked of Henry, "since her removal?"

"Anxious still," said Henry; "but I think, better."

"That is well. I perceive that, naturally, we are all three walking towards Bannerworth Hall, and perhaps it is as well that it be there that I should ask you, Henry, to indulge me with a confidence such as, under ordinary circumstances, I should not at all feel myself justified in requiring of you."

"To what does it relate?" asked Henry. "You may be assured, Mr. Chillingworth, that I am not likely to refuse my confidence to you, whom I have so much reason to respect as an attached friend of myself and my family."

"You will not object, I hope," added Mr. Chillingworth, "to extending that confidence to Admiral Bell, for as you well know, a truer and more warm-hearted man than he does not exist."

"What do you expect for that, doctor?" asked the Admiral.

"There is nothing," said Henry, "that I could relate at all that I should shrink from relating to Admiral Bell."

"Well said, my boy," said the Admiral, "and all I can reply to that is that you are quite right, for there can be nothing that you need shrink from telling me, you may trust my digression with anything you choose to tell me."

"I am assured of that."

"A British officer, once pledging his word, prefers death to breaking it. Whatever you wish kept secret in the communication you make to me, say so, and it will never pass my lips."

"Why, sir, the fact is that what I am about to relate to you consists of secrets about matters which would be painful to my feelings to talk of more than may be absolutely required."

"I understand you."

"Let me, for a moment," said Mr. Chillingworth, "put myself right. I do not suspect, Mr. Henry Bannerworth, that you fancy I ask you to make a recital of the circumstances of your father's death which must be painful to you from any idle motive. But let me declare that I have now a stronger impulse, which induces me to wish to hear from your own lips those matters which popular rumor may have greatly exaggerated."

"It is scarcely possible," sadly remarked Henry, "that popular rumor should exaggerate the facts."

"Indeed!"

"No. They are unhappily in their bare truthfulness, so full of all that can be grievous to those who are in any way connected with them, that there needs no exaggeration to invest them with more terror, or with more of that sadness which must ever belong to a recollection of them in my mind."

The time was passed in suchlike discourse until Henry Bannerworth and his friends once more reached the Hall, from which he, with his family, had so recently removed in consequence of the fearful persecution to which they had been subjected.

They passed again into the garden which they all knew so well, and then Henry paused and looked around him with a deep sigh.

In answer to an inquiring glance from Mr. Chillingworth, he said, "Is it not strange, now that I should have only been away from here a space of time which may be counted by hours, and yet all seems changed. I could almost fancy that years had elapsed since I had looked at it."

"Oh," remarked the doctor, "time is always measured by the number of events which are crowded into a given space of it, and not by its actual duration. Come into the house; there you will find all just as you left it, Henry, and you can tell us your story at leisure."

"The air," Henry said, "is fresh and pleasant here. Let us sit down in the summer-house yonder, and there I will tell you all. It has a local interest, too, connected with this tale."

This was agreed to, and in a few moments the Admiral, Mr. Chillingworth, and Henry were seated in the same summer-house which had witnessed the strange interview between Sir Francis Varney and Flora Bannerworth in which he had induced her to believe that he felt for the distress he had occasioned her, and was strongly impressed with the injustice of her sufferings.

Henry was silent for some moments, and then he said with a deep sigh as he looked mournfully around him, "It was on this spot that my father breathed his last, and hence have I said that it has a local interest in the tale I have to tell, which makes it the most fitting place in which to tell it."

"Oh?" said the Admiral; "he died here, did he?"

"Yes, where you are now sitting."

"Very good; I have seen many a brave man die in my time, and I hope to see a few more; although I grant you the death in the heat of conflict and fighting for our country is a vastly different thing to some shore-going mode of leaving the world."

"Yes," said Henry as if pursuing his own meditation rather than listening to the Admiral. "Yes, it was from this precise spot that my father took his last look at the family house. What we can now see of it, he saw of it with his dying eyes, and many a time I have sat here and fancied the world of terrible thoughts that must at such a moment have come across his brain."

"You might well do so," said the doctor.

"You can see," added Henry, "that from here the fullest view you have of any of the windows of the house is of that of Flora's room, as we have always called it, because for years she had it as her chamber. You, doctor," added Henry, "who know much of my family, need not be told what sort of man my father was."

"No, indeed."

"But you, Admiral Bell, who do not know, must be told, and, however grievous it may be for me to have to say so, I must inform you that he was not a man who would have merited your esteem."

"Well," the Admiral observed, "you know, my boy, that can make no difference regarding you in anybody's mind. Every man's credit, character, and honor, to my thinking is in his own most special keeping. Let your father be what he might, or who he might, I do not see that any conduct of his ought to raise upon your cheek the flush of shame, or cost you more uneasiness than ordinary good feeling dictates to the errors and feelings of a fellow creature."

"If all of the world, would take such liberal and comprehensive views as you do, Admiral, it would be much happier than it is, but such is not the case. People are all too apt to blame one person for the evil that another has done."

"Ah, but," Mr. Chillingworth stated, "it so happens that those are the people whose opinions are of the very least consequence."

"There is some truth in that," Henry said sadly; "but let me proceed; since I have to tell the tale, I could wish the telling over. My father,

The Flight Of The Vampyre

Admiral Bell, although a man not tainted in early life with vices, became by the force of bad associates, and a sort of want of congeniality and sentiment that sprang up between him and my mother, plunged into all the excesses of his age.

"These excesses were all of that character which the most readily lay hold strongly of an unreflecting mind, because they all presented themselves in the garb of sociality. The wine cup is drained in the name of good fellowship; money which is wanted for legitimate purposes is squandered under the mask of a noble and free generosity, and all that the small imagination of a number of persons of perverted intellects could enable them to do, has been done from time to time, to impart a kind of luster to intemperance and all its dreadful and criminal consequences.

"My father, having once wandered into the company of what he considered wits and men of spirit[xx], soon became thoroughly a part of it. He was almost the only one of the set who was really worth anything, monetarily speaking. There were some among them who might have been respectable men and perchance earned their way to fortune as well as some others who had started in life with good inheritances, but my father, at the time he became associated with them, was the only one, as I say whom, to use a phrase I have heard myself from his lips concerning them, had got a feather to fly with.

"The consequence of this was that his society, merely for gratification of drinking at his expense, was courted, and he was much flattered, all of which he laid to the score of his own merits, which had been found out and duly appreciated by these *bon vivants*, while he considered that the grave admonitions of his real friends proceeded from nothing in the world but downright envy and malice. Such a state of things as this could not last very long. The associates of my father wanted money as well as wine, so they introduced him to the gaming-table, and he became fascinated with the fearful vice to an extent which predicted his own destruction and the ruin of everyone who was in any way dependent upon him.

"He could not sell Bannerworth Hall unless I gave my consent, which I refused, but he accumulated debt upon debt, and from time to time stripped the mansion of all its most costly contents.

"With various mutations of fortune he continued this horrible and destructive career for a long time, until at last he found himself utterly and irretrievably ruined, and he came home in an agony of despair, being so weak and physically exhausted that he kept his bed for many days.

"It appeared that something occurred at this juncture which gave him a hope that he should possess some money, and be again in a position to try his fortune at the gaming-table. He rose and, fortifying himself once more with the strong stimulations of wine and spirits, he left his home and was absent for about two months.

"What occurred to him during that time none of us ever knew, but late one night he came home, apparently much flurried in manner, and seeming as if something had happened to drive him half mad.

"Shutting himself up the whole of the night in the chamber where hangs the portrait that bears so strong a resemblance to Sir Francis Varney, he would not speak to anyone, and there he remained till the morning when he emerged and said briefly that he intended to leave the country.

"He was in a most fearful state of nervousness, and my mother tells me that he shook like someone in a fever, and jumped at every little sound that occurred in the house, and glared about him so wildly that it was horrible to see him or to sit in the same apartment with him. She says that the whole morning passed on in this way 'till a letter came to him, the contents of which appeared to throw him into a perfect convulsion of terror, and he retired again to the room with the portrait where he remained some hours, and then he emerged, looking like a ghost, dreadfully pale and haggard.

"He walked into the garden here, and was observed sitting down in this summer-house, his eyes fixed upon the window of that apartment." Henry paused for a few moments, and then he added. "You will excuse me from entering upon any details of what ensued next in the melancholy history. My father committed suicide here. He was found dying, and all the words he spoke were, "The money is hidden!" Death claimed his victim, and, with a convulsive spasm, he resigned his spirit, leaving what he had intended to say hidden in the oblivion of the grave.

"That was an odd affair," indicated the Admiral.

"It was, indeed. We have all pondered deeply, and the result was that, upon the whole, we were inclined to come to an opinion that the words he so uttered were the result of the mental disturbance that at such a moment might well be supposed to be ensuing in the mind, and that they related really to no foregone fact any more than some incoherent words uttered by a man in a dream might be supposed to do so."

"It may be so."

"I do not mean," Mr. Chillingworth remarked, "for one moment to attempt to dispute, Henry, the rationality of such an opinion as you have just given utterance to, but you forget that another circumstance occurred, which gave a color to the words used by your father."

"Yes; I know to what you allude."

"Be so good at to state it to the Admiral."

"I will. On the evening of that same day there a man here who asked to see my father, seemingly ignorance of what had occurred, although by that time it was well known to all the neighborhood. Upon being told that he was dead, he started back, either with well acted or with real surprise, and seemed to be immensely chagrined. He then demanded to know if he had left any disposition of his property, but he got no information and departed muttering the most diabolical oaths and curses that can be imagined. He mounted his horse, for he had ridden to the Hall, and his last words were, as I am told, "Where, in the name of all that's damnable can he have put the money?'"

"And did you ever find out who this man was?" asked the Admiral.

"Never."

"It is an odd affair."

"It is," said Mr. Chillingworth, "and full of mystery. The public mind was much taken up at the time with some other matters, or it would have made the death of Mr. Bannerworth the subject of more prolific comment than it did. As it was, however, a great deal was said upon the subject, and the whole county was in a state of commotion for weeks afterwards."

"Yes," said Henry; "it so happened that about that very time a murder was committed in the neighborhood of London which baffled all the exertions of the authorities to discover the perpetrators of. It was the murder of Lord Lorne."

"Oh! I remember," exclaimed the Admiral; "the newspapers were full of it for a long time."

"As Mr. Chillingworth says, the more exciting interest of that affair drew off public attention, in a great measure, from my father's suicide, and we did not suffer so much from public remark and from impertinent curiosity as might otherwise have been expected."

"And, in addition," said Mr. Chillingworth, and he changed color a little as he spoke, "there was an execution shortly afterwards."

"Yes," said Henry, "there was."

"The execution of a man named Angerstein," added Mr. Chillingworth, "for a highway robbery perpetrated with the most brutal violence."

"True; all the affairs of that period of time are strongly impressed upon my mind," said Henry; "but you do not seem well, Mr. Chillingworth."

"Oh, yes; I am quite well – you are mistaken."

Both the Admiral and Henry looked at the doctor, who certainly appeared to them to be laboring under some great mental excitement which he found it almost beyond his power to repress.

"I tell you what it is, doctor," said the Admiral; "I don't pretend to see any further than my neighbors, but I can see far enough to feel convinced that you have got something on your mind, and that it somehow concerns this affair."

"Is it so?" asked Henry.

"I cannot say what it is, even if I would," said Mr. Chillingworth in an confounded manner; "and I may with truth add, that I would not hide from you that I have something on my mind connected with this affair, but let me assure you it would be premature of me to tell you of it."

"Premature be damned!" roared the Admiral; "out with it."

"Nay, nay, dear sir; I am not now in a position to say what is passing through my mind."

"Alter your position, then, and be blowed!" cried Jack Pringle, suddenly stepping forward and giving the doctor such a push that he nearly went through one of the sides of the summer-house.

"Why, you scoundrel!" cried the Admiral, "how came you here?"

"On my legs," said Jack. "Do you think nobody wants to know nothing but yourself? I'm as fond of a yarn as anybody."

"But if you are," said Mr. Chillingworth, "you had no occasion to come against me as if you wanted to move a house."

"You said as you wasn't in a position to say something as I wanted to hear, so I thought I'd alter your position for you."

"Is this fellow," the doctor asked, shaking his head as he accosted the Admiral, "the most artful or stupid?"

"A little of both," said Admiral Bell; "a little of both, doctor. He's a great fool and a great scamp."

"The same to you," said Jack; "you're another. I shall hate you presently if you go on making yourself so ridiculous. Now, mind, I'll only give you a trial of another week or so, and if you don't be more polite in your damn language, I'll leave you."

Away strolled Jack towards the house with his hands in his pockets, while the Admiral was half choked with rage, and could only glare after him without the ability to say a word.

Under any other circumstances than the present one of trouble and difficulty and deep anxiety, Henry Bannerworth must have laughed at these singular little episodes between Jack and the Admiral, but his mind was now by far too much harassed to permit him to do so.

"Let him go, let him go, my dear sir," Mr. Chillingworth told the Admiral, who showed some signs of an intention to pursue Jack; "he no doubt has been drinking again."

"I'll turn him off the first moment I catch him sober enough to understand me," raged the Admiral.

"Well, well; do as you please, but now let me ask a favor of both of you."

"What is it?"

"That you will leave Bannerworth Hall to me for a week."

"What for?"

"I hope to make some discoveries connected with it which shall well reward you for the trouble."

"It's no trouble," said Henry; "and for myself, I have sufficient faith, both in your judgment and in your friendship, doctor, to accede to any request which you may make to me."

"And I," said the Admiral. "Be it so – be it so. For one week, you say?"

"Yes – for one week. I hope, by the end of that time, to have achieved something worth the telling of, and I promise you that, if I am at all disappointed in my expecting, that I will frankly and freely communicate to you all I know and all I suspect."

"Then that's a bargain."

"It is."

"And what's to be done at once?"

"Why, nothing but to take the greatest possible care that Bannerworth Hall is not left another hour without someone in it, and in order that such should be the case, I have to request that you two will remain here until I go to the town and make preparations for taking quiet possession of it myself, which I will do in the course of two hours, at most."

"Don't be longer," said the Admiral, "for I am so desperately hungry that I shall certainly begin to eat somebody if you are any longer than that."

"Depend upon me."

"Very well," said Henry; "you may depend that we will wait here until you come back."

The doctor at once hurried from the garden, leaving Henry and the Admiral to amuse themselves as best they might with conjectures as to what he was really about, until his return.

Chapter 62
The Mysterious Meeting in the Ruin Again – The Vampyre's Attack upon the Constable

It is now necessary that we return once more to that mysterious ruin to which Varney had fled when pursued by the mob, where he had found a refuge which defied all the attempts to find him. Our readers must be well aware, by now, that connected with that ruin are some secrets of great importance to our story, and we will now – at the solemn hour of midnight – take another glance at what is happening within its dank and dreary recesses.

At that solemn hour it is not likely that anyone would seek that gloomy place out of choice. Some lover of the picturesque might visit it in glorious daylight in order to sketch the progression of man's ruin, but such was not the cause of the pilgrimage for those who were soon to stand within its gloomy precincts.

Other motives dictated their presence in that spot.

As the neighboring clocks sounded the hour of midnight, and the faint sounds were borne gently on the wind to that isolated ruin, a tall man could be observed standing by the porch.

His form was enveloped in a large cloak which was of such ample material that he could easily wrap it several times around him, and even then leave a considerable portion of it floating idly in the gentle wind.

He stood as still, as calm, and as motionless as a statue for a considerable time, before any degree of impatience began to show itself. Then he took from his pocket a large antique watch, the white face just enabling him to see what the time was, and in a voice which had in it some amount of petulance and anger, he fumed, "Not here yet, and nearly half an hour beyond the time! What can have detained him? This is, indeed, trifling with the most important moments of a man's existence."

Even as he spoke, he heard from some distance off the sound of a short, quick footstep. He bent forward to listen, and then, in a tone of satisfaction, he said, "He comes – he comes!"

But this mysterious figure waiting for some confederate among these dim and old grey ruins did not advance a step to meet him. On the contrary, such seemed the amount of cold-blooded caution which he possessed, that the nearer the man – who was evidently advancing – got to the place, the further back did our shadowy man shrink into the shadow of the dim and rumbling walls.

And yet, surely he need not have been so cautious. Who was likely to come to the ruins at such an unlikely hour but the one who came for an appointment?

And, moreover, the manner of the advancing man should have been quite sufficient to convince him who waited that so much caution was unnecessary, but it was a part and parcel of his nature.

About three minutes more sufficed to bring the second man to the ruin, and he, at once and fearlessly, plunged into its recesses.

"Who comes?" the first man asked in a deep, hollow voice.

"He whom you expect," was the reply.

"Good," he said emerging from his hiding-place; soon they stood together in the nearly total darkness with which the place was enshrouded, for the night was a cloudy one and there appeared not a star in the heavens to shed its faint light upon the scene below.

For a few moments they were both silent, for the man who had lately arrived had evidently made great exertions to reach the spot and was breathing laboriously, while he who was there first appeared, from some natural taciturnity of character, to decline opening the conversation.

At length the second comer spoke, saying, "I have made some exertion to get here on time, and yet I am still late as you are no doubt aware."

"Yes, yes."

"Well, such would not have been the case, but I stayed to bring you some news of importance."

"Well, let's hear it then."

"This place, which we have had for some time as a quiet and perfectly eligible one for our meetings is about to be invaded by one of those restless, troublesome spirits, who are never happy except when they are contriving something to the annoyance of others who do not interfere with them."

"Explain yourself more fully; what has occurred?"

"At a tavern in the town some strange scenes of violence have occurred because of the general excitement which the common people have been thrown into over the dreadful subject of vampyres. The consequence of the uproar is that the offenders have broken into the inn to drive a stake through the body of a passerby who happened to die during his stay at the inn. They have unburied the body of the butcher, who happened to die also, recently of some sort of wasting trouble. The Dragoons have been called, and numerous arrests have taken place, and the places to confine the offenders are now full of those country-folk whose heated and angry imaginations have caused them to take violent steps to discover the reality or the falsehood of rumors which so much affected them, their wives, and their families, that they feared to lie down to their night's repose."

The other figure laughed a short, hollow, restless sort of laugh, one which had not one particle of real mirth in it.

"Go on – go on," he said. "What else did they do?"

"As I said, immense excesses have been committed, but what made me late was that I overheard a man declaring his intention this night, from twelve till the morning, and for some nights to come, to hold watch and ward for the vampyre."

"Did he indeed!"

"Yes. It was only at the earnest solicitation of his comrades that he take yet another glass, before he came upon his expedition, that I have arrived before him."

"He must be met. The idiot! What business is this of his?"

"There are always people who will make everything their business, whether it is so or not."

"There are always far too many of this sort of being. Let us retire further into the recesses of this ruin, and there consider what action is to be done about such a rash intruder to this place."

They both walked for twenty paces or so, right into the ruin, and then he who had been there first, said, suddenly, to his companion, "I am annoyed that my reputation has spread so widely, and made so much noise."

"Your reputation as Varney, the vampyre?"

"Yes, but you don't need to utter my name aloud, even here where we are alone together."

"It came out unawares," the newcomer quickly interjected.

"Unawares!" Varney exclaimed forcefully. "Can it be possible that you have so little command over yourself as to allow a name to come from your lips unawares?"

"Sometimes."

"Well, it cannot be helped; it is said. What do you now propose to do?"

"You are my private councilor. Have you no deep-laid, artful project in hand? Can you not plan for, and arrange something, which may still make it possible to accomplish my goals, which at first seemed so very simple, but which have recently become full of difficulty and danger?"

"I must confess I have no plan."

"I am astonished."

"Nay, now you are jesting."

"When did you ever hear of me jesting?"

"Not often, I admit. I have always" Varney added, "found it easier to be the person who performs the plan than to plan an elaborate course of action for others to perform."

"Then you throw it all on me?"

"I throw a weight, naturally enough, upon the shoulders which I think the best adapted to sustain it."

"Be it so, then – be it so."

"You are, I presume from what you say, able to come up with a scheme of action which shall present better hopes of success, I hope. Look what great danger we have already passed through."

"Yes, we have."

"It is not the danger that annoys and troubles me, but it is that, notwithstanding the danger, our goal is still far off."

"Not only that, we have made it more difficult to obtain what we want by alerting the very people who are most likely to oppose us."

"That we have," agreed Varney.

"And we have placed the probability of success further away."

"And yet I have set my life upon the case, and I will stand the hazard. I tell you I will accomplish this object, I will find the treasure hidden in the Hall, or I will perish in the attempt."

"You are too enthusiastic."

"Not at all. Nothing has been ever done that was difficult to accomplish, without enthusiasm. I will do what I intend, or Bannerworth Hall shall become a heap of ruins where fire shall do its worst work of devastation, and I will myself find a grave in the midst."

"Well, I quarrel with no man for chalking out the course he intends to pursue," Varney maintained, "but what do you mean to do with the prisoner below here?"

"Kill him," the stranger said.

"What?"

"I say, kill him. What part do you not understand? When everything else is secured, and I have that which I seek secure in my possession, I will take his life, or you shall. There shall be no danger in taking the life of a man who is chained to the floor of a dungeon."

"I don't know why, you take a pleasure on this particular night, of all others, in saying all you can which you think will be offensive to me."

"Psha! That Admiral is the great stumbling-block in my way. I should have had undisturbed possession of Bannerworth Hall before this except for him. He must be got out of the way somehow."

"A short time will tire him with keeping watch. He is one of those men of impulse who soon become wearied of inaction."

"Ay, but then the Bannerworths may return to the Hall."

"It may be so."

"I am certain of it. We have been outmaneuvered in this matter; although, we did all that men could do to give us success."

"In what way would you get rid of this troublesome Admiral?"

"I scarcely know. A letter from his nephew might, if well put together, get him to London. But I doubt it. I hate him mortally," the newcomer stated vehemently. "He has offended me more than once most grievously."

"I know it." Varney agreed before continuing dryly, "He saw through you."

The Flight Of The Vampyre

"I do not give him so much credit. He is a suspicious man, and a vain and jealous one."

"And yet he saw through you. Now, listen to me. You are completely at fault, and have no plan of operations whatever in your mind. What I want you to do is to disappear from the neighborhood for a while, and so will I. As for our prisoner here below, I cannot see what else can be done with him than – than…"

"Than to dispose of him? Do you hesitate?"

"I do."

"Then what is it you were about to say?"

"I cannot but feel that all we have done, hitherto, as regards this young prisoner of ours, has failed. He has, with a determined obstinacy, set at naught all threats. He has refused to do any action which could in any way aid me in my objects. In fact, from the first to the last, he has been nothing but an expense and a bother to us both."

"And yet, although you and I both know of an easy way to get rid of such distractions, I must own that I feel a certain sense of reluctance to the murder of the youth."

"You have seriously considered the necessity, then?" asked the other.

"And you have not considered it?" Varney inquired dryly.

"I have no such wish, and what is more, I not will be the one to do it."

"Then we shall not murder the youth; only the question then remains, what shall we do with him? It is far easier in all enterprises to decide upon what we will not do than upon what we will."

"Listen. I will not have the life of Charles Holland taken."

"Who wishes to take it?"

"You hinted rather strongly that you would be grateful should I do so."

"There, indeed, you wrong me. Do you think that I would needlessly bring down upon my head the odium, as well as the danger, of such a deed? No, no. Let him live, if you are willing; he may live a thousand years for all I care."

"'Tis well. I am determined that he shall live, so far as we are concerned. I can respect the courage that allowed him, even when he considered that his life was at stake, to say no to a proposal which was cowardly and dishonorable, although it went far to the defeat of my own plans and has involved me in much trouble."

"Hush! hush!"

"What is it?"

"I think I hear a footstep."

"A footstep would be a novelty in such a place as this."

"And yet this intrusion is what I expected. Have you forgotten what I told you when I reached here to-night after the appointed hour?"

"Truly; I had for the moment. Do you think then that the footstep is that of the adventurer who boasted that he could keep watch for the vampyre?"

"Yes I do. What is to be done with such a meddling fool?"

"He certainly should be taught not to be so fond of interfering with other people's affairs."

"He certainly should be!"

"Perchance the lesson will not be wholly thrown away upon others. It may be worthwhile to take some trouble with the drunken, valiant fellow, and let him spread his news so as to stop anyone else from being equally venturous and troublesome."

"A good thought."

"Shall it be done?"

"Yes; if you will arrange something that shall accomplish such a result."

"Be it so. The moon rises."

"It does."

"Ah, already I fancy I see a brightening of the air. Come further within the ruins."

They both walked further among the crumbling walls and fragments of columns with which the place abounded. As they did so, they paused now and then to listen, and more than once they both plainly heard the sound of certain footsteps outside the once handsome and spacious building.

Varney, the vampyre, who had been holding this conversation with no other than Mr. Marchdale, who was the mysterious stranger, smiled as he, in a whispered voice, told the latter what to do in order to frighten the foolhardy man away from the place in which he wandered, thinking that thinking that by himself he would be able to accomplish something against the vampyre.

It was, indeed, a harebrained expedition, for whether Sir Francis Varney was really so awful and preternatural a being as so many confirmatory circumstances would seem to proclaim, or not, he was not a likely being to allow himself to be conquered by any one individual, let his powers or his courage be what they might.

What induced this man to become so venturesome we shall now proceed to relate, as well as what kind of reception he got in the old ruins, which, since the mysterious disappearance of Sir Francis Varney within their recesses, had possessed so increased a share of interest and attracted so much popular attention and speculation.

Chapter 63
The Guests at the Inn – And the Story of the Dead Uncle

As had been stated by Mr. Marchdale, who now stands out in his true colors to the reader as the confidant and aid of Sir Francis Varney, there had assembled on that evening a curious and gossiping party at the inn where the dreadful proceedings had taken place which we have already duly and at length imparted.

It was not very likely that on that evening, or for many and many an evening to come, the conversation in the parlor of the inn would be about any subject other than that of the vampyre.

Indeed, the strange, mysterious, and horrible circumstances which had occurred bade fair to be prime gossip for many a year; never before had a topic of conversation presenting so many curious features arisen.

Everybody might have his individual opinion and be just as likely to be right as his neighbors, and the beauty of the affair was that the subject itself was so interesting that there was sure to be some spot of interest with every surmise which could be created by even the most fervent imagination.

On this particular night when Marchdale was prowling about and gathering what news he could in order that he might carry it to the vampyre, a more than usually strong muster of the gossips of the town took place.

Indeed, all the local master gossips were gathered there, with the exception of one, and he was in the county jail, having been one of the prisoners apprehended by the military when they made the successful attack upon the attic of the inn after the dreadful desecration of the dead which had taken place.

The Flight Of The Vampyre

The landlord of the inn was likely to make a good thing of it, for talking makes people thirsty, and he began to consider that a vampyre about once-a-year would be a good thing for the Blue Lion.

"It's shocking," said one of the guests; "it's shocking to think of. Only last night, I am quite sure I had such a fright that it took at least ten years off my age."

"A fright!" a chorus of voices answered the claim.

"I believe I speak English – I said a fright."

"Well, had it anything to do with the vampyre?"

"Everything," he said portentously.

"Oh! Do tell us; do tell us all about it. How was it? Did he come to you? Go on. Well, well."

The first speaker became immediately a very important person in the room, and when he was that, he became at once a very important person in his own eyes and, before he would speak another word, he filled a fresh pipe and ordered another mug of ale.

"It's no use trying to hurry him," said one.

"No," he said, "it isn't. I'll tell you in good time what a dreadful circumstance has made me sixty-three today, when I was only fifty-three yesterday."

"Was it very dreadful?"

"Rather. You wouldn't have survived at all."

"Indeed!"

"No. Now listen. I went to bed at a quarter after eleven as usual. I didn't notice anything particular in the room."

"Did you peep under the bed?"

"No, I didn't. Well, as I was a-saying, to bed I went, and I didn't fasten the door; because, being a very sound sleeper, in case there was a fire, I shouldn't hear a word of it if I did."

"No," began another. "I recollect once…"

"Be so good as to allow me to finish what I know, before you begin to recollect anything, if you please. As I was saying, I didn't lock the door, but I went to bed. Somehow or another, I did not feel at all comfortable, and I tossed about, first on one side and then on the other, but it was all in vain; I only got, every moment, more and more fidgety."

"And did you think of the vampyre?" asked one of the listeners.

"I thought of nothing else till I heard my clock, which is on the landing of the stairs above my bed-room, begin to strike twelve."

The Flight Of The Vampyre

"Ah! I like to hear a clock sound in the night," said one; "it puts one in mind of the rest of the world, and lets one know one isn't all alone."

"Very good. The striking of the clock I should not at all have objected to, but it was what followed that did the business."

"What, what?"

"Fair and softly; fair and softly. Just hand me a light, Mr. Sprigs, if you please. I'll tell you all, gentlemen, in a moment or two."

With the most provoking deliberation the speaker relit his pipe, which had gone out while he was talking, and then, after a few whiffs to assure himself that its contents had thoroughly ignited, he resumed, "No sooner had the last sound of it died away than I heard something on the stairs."

"Yes, yes, what was it you heard?" asked one of the more impatient listeners.

"It was as if some man had knocked his foot hard against one of the stairs, and he would have needed to have had a heavy boot on to do it. I started up in bed and listened, as you may well suppose, and then I heard an odd, gnawing sort of noise, and then another knock upon one of the stairs."

"How dreadful!"

"It was. I had no idea what to do, or what to think; I thought the vampyre had gotten in at the attic window, and was coming down stairs to my room. That seemed most likely. Then there was another groan, and then another heavy step, and, as they were evidently coming towards my door, I got out of bed and went to try and lock my door."

There was muttered agreement and nods among the listeners that this was the most sensible reaction to such a circumstance.

"Yes; that was all very well, if I could have done it, but I shook from head to foot. The room was very dark, and I couldn't, for a moment or two, collect my senses sufficient really to know which way the door lay."

"What a situation!"

"It was. Dab, dab, dab, came these horrid footsteps, and there was I groping about the room in an agony. I heard them coming nearer and nearer to my door. Another moment and they must have reached it, when my hand struck against the lock."

"What an escape!"

"No, it was not."

"No?"

"No, indeed. The key was on the outside, and you may well guess I was not disposed to open the door to get at it."

He now had his listeners in the palm of his hand. One of them was so moved that he handed a fresh drink to the speaker; who continued, "I felt regularly bewildered, I can tell you; it seemed to me as if the very devil himself was coming down stairs hopping all the way upon one leg."

"How terrifying!"

"I felt my senses almost leaving me. But I did what I could to hold the door shut just as I heard the strange step come from the last stair on to the landing. Then there was a horrid sound, and someone began trying the lock of my door."

"What a moment!"

"Yes, I can tell you it was a moment, such a moment as I don't wish to go through again. I held the door as closed as I could, and did not speak. I tried to cry out 'help' and 'murder,' but I could not; my tongue stuck to the roof of my mouth and my strength was fast failing me."

"Horrid, horrid!"

"Take a drop of ale," another urged him.

"Thank you. Well, I don't think this went on above two or three minutes, and all the while someone tried with might and main to push open the door. My strength left me all at once; I had only time to stagger back a step or two, and then, as the door opened, I fainted away."

"Well, well!"

"Ah, you wouldn't have said well if you had been there, I can tell you."

"No, but what become of you. What happened next? How did it end? What was it?"

"Why, what exactly happened next after I fainted I cannot tell you, but the first thing I saw when I recovered was a candle."

"Yes, yes."

"And then a crowd of people."

"Ah, ah!"

"And then Dr. Webb."

"Gracious!"

"And Mrs. Bulk, my housekeeper. I was in my own bed, and when I opened my eyes I heard Dr. Webb say, '"He will be better soon. Can no one suggest any idea of what it is all about? Some sudden fright surely alone could not have produced such an effect."

"The Lord have mercy upon me!" I said. "Upon this, everybody who had been called in got round the bed, and wanted to know what had happened, but I said not a word of it, but turning to Mrs. Bulk, I asked her how it was she found out I had fainted.

"Why, sir," says she, "I was coming up to bed as softly as I could because I knew you had gone to rest some time before. The clock was striking twelve, and as I went past it some of my clothes, I suppose, caught the large weight, and it was knocked off, and down the stairs it rolled, going with such a lump from one to the other, and I couldn't catch it because it rolled so fast, that I made sure you would be awakened; so I came down to tell you what it was, and it was some time before I could get your room door open, and when I did I found you out of bed and insensible.'"

There was a general look and sound of disappointment when this explanation was given, and one said, "Then it was not the vampire?"

"Certainly not."

"And, after all, only a clock weight."

"That's about it."

"Why didn't you tell us about that at first?"

"Because that would have spoilt the story."

There was a general murmur of discontent, and, after a few moments one man said, with some vivacity, "Well, although our friend's vampyre has turned out to be nothing but a confounded clock-weight, there's no disputing the fact about Sir Francis Varney being a vampyre and not a clock-weight."

"Very true – very true."

"And what's to be done to rid the town of such a man?"

"Oh, don't call him a man."

"Well, a monster."

"Ah, that's more like." Turning to the story-teller he added, "I tell you what, sir, if you had got a light when you first heard the noise in your room and gone out to see what it was, you would have spared yourself much fright."

"Ah, no doubt; it's always easy afterwards to say, if you had done this, and if you had done the other, so and so would have been the effect, but there is something about the hour of midnight that makes men tremble."

"Well," said one, who had not yet spoken and who always disposed to argue with anyone, "I don't see why twelve at night should be any more disagreeable than twelve at day."

"Don't you?"

"Not I," he averred.

"Now, for instance, many a party of pleasure goes to that old ruin where Sir Francis Varney so unaccountably disappeared in broad daylight. But is there anyone here who would go to it alone, and at midnight?"

"Yes."

"Who?"

"I would."

"What! And after what has happened as regards the vampyre in connection with it?"

"Yes, I would."

"I'll bet you twenty shillings you won't."

"And I – and I," cried several.

"Well, gentlemen," said the man, who certainly showed no signs of fear, "I will go, and not only will I go and take all your bets, but, if I do meet the vampyre, then I'll do my best to take him prisoner."

"And when will you go?"

"To-night," he cried springing to his feet; "hark ye all, I don't believe one word about a vampyre. I'll go at once; it's getting late, and let one of you, in order that you may be convinced I have really been to the place, give me an article which I will hide among the ruins, and tell you where to find it tomorrow in broad daylight."

"Well," said one, "that's fair, Tom Eccles. Here's a handkerchief of mine; I should know it again among a hundred others."

"Agreed; I'll leave it in the ruins."

The wagers were fairly agreed upon, and several handkerchiefs were handed to Tom Eccles, and at eleven o'clock he started through the murky darkness of the night to the old ruin where Sir Francis Varney and Mr. Marchdale were holding their most unholy conference.

It is one thing to talk and to accept wagers in the snug parlor of an inn, and another to go alone across a tract of country wrapped in the profound stillness of night to an ancient ruin which, in addition to the natural gloom which might well be supposed to surround it, has superadded associations which are of anything but a pleasant character.

Tom Eccles was one of those individuals who allow impulse to govern their actions. He was certainly not a coward, and perhaps really as free from superstition as most persons, but he was human and consequently he had nerves, and he had likewise imagination.

He went to his house before he departed on his errand to the ruins. It was to get a horse-pistol which he duly loaded and placed in his pocket. Then he wrapped himself up in a great-coat, and with the air of a man quite determined upon performing some desperate action, he left the town.

The guests at the inn looked after him as he walked from the door of that friendly establishment, and some of them, as they saw his resolved aspect, began to quake for the amount of the wagers they had laid upon his non-success.

However, it was resolved among them to wait until half-past twelve in the expectation of his return, before they separated.

To while away the time, he who had been so facetious about his story of the clock-weight, volunteered to tell what happened to a friend of his who went to take possession of some family property which he became possessed of as heir-at-law to an uncle who had died without a will, leaving his illegitimate family unprovided for in every shape.

"Go on – let's know all about it," his friends clamored, for they really enjoyed his story-telling.

"Well, as I was saying, or about to say, the nephew, as soon as he heard his uncle was dead, comes and puts everything in the house under lock and key."

"But, could he do so?" inquired one of the guests.

"I don't see what was to hinder him," replied a third. "He could do so, certainly."

"But there was a son and, as I take it, a son's nearer than a nephew any day."

"But the son is illegitimate."

"Legitimate, or illegitimate, a son's a son; don't bother me about distinction of that sort; why, now, there was old Weatherbit…"

"Order, order."

"Let's hear the tale."

"Very good, gentlemen, I'll go on if I ain't to be interrupted, but I'll say this, that an illegitimate son is no son in the eyes of the law, or at most he's an accident, quite, and ain't what he is, and so can't inherit."

"Well, that's what I call making matters plain," said one of the guests, who took his pipe from his mouth to make room for the remark; "now that is what I likes."

"Well, as I have told you then," resumed the speaker, "the nephew was the heir, and into the house he would come. A fine affair it was too – the illegitimates looking pretty grim, but he knew the law, and would have it put in force."

"Law's law, you know."

"Uncommonly true that the law is a thing unto itself, and the nephew stuck to the law – he said they should be put out, and they did go out and, say what they would about their natural claims, he would not listen to them, but bundled them out in a pretty short space of time."

"It was trying to them, mind you, to leave the house they had been born in with very different expectations to those which now appeared to be their fate. Poor things, they looked ruefully enough, and well they might, for there was a wide world for them, and no prospect of a warm corner."

"Well, as I was saying, he had them all out, and the house clear to himself.

"Now," said he, "I have an open field. I don't care for no – Eh! what!"

"There was a sudden knocking at the door, and he went and opened it, but nothing was to be seen."

"Oh, I see – somebody next door must have knocked, and if it wasn't them it don't matter. There's nobody here. I'm alone, and there are plenty of valuables in the house. That is what I call very good company. I wouldn't wish for better."

He turned about, looked over room after room, and satisfied himself that he was alone – that the house was empty.

As he entered each room, he paused to think over the value – what it was worth, and that he was a very fortunate man in having dropped into such a good thing."

"Ah! There's the old boy's desk, too – his bureau – there'll be something in that that will amuse me mightily, but I don't think I shall sit up late. He was a rum old man, to say the least of it – a very odd sort of man." With that he gave himself a shrug, as if some very uncomfortable feeling had come over him.

The Flight Of The Vampyre

"I'll go to bed early and get some sleep, and then in daylight I can look after these papers. They won't be less interesting in the morning than they are now."

There was some odd stories about the old man, and now the nephew thought that he should have let the family sleep on the premises for that night; yes, at that moment he could have found it in his heart to have paid for all the expense of their keep had it been possible to have had them back to remain the night.

The night came on, and he had lights. It was true that he had not been downstairs, only just to have a look. He could not tell what sort of a place it was; there were a good many odd sort of passages that seemed to end nowhere.

He then went upstairs and sat down in the room where the bureau was placed.

"I'll be bound," said one of the guests, "He was in a bit of a stew, notwithstanding all his brag."

"Oh! I don't believe," said another, "that anything done that is dangerous, or supposed to be dangerous, by the bravest man, is in any way wholly without some uncomfortable feelings. They may not be strong enough to prevent the thing proposed to be done from being done, but they give a disagreeable sensation to the skin."

"You have felt it, then?"

"Ha! ha! ha!"

"Why, that time I slept in the churchyard for a wager, I must say I felt cold all over, as if my skin was walking about me in an uncomfortable manner."

"But you won your wager?"

"I did."

"And of course you slept there?"

"To be sure I did."

"And met with nothing?"

"Nothing except a few bumps against the gravestones."

"Those were hard knocks, I should say."

"They were, I assure you, but I lay there, and slept there, and won my wager."

"Would you do it again?"

"No."

"And why not?"

"Because of the rheumatism?"

"You caught that?"

"I did; I would give ten times my wager to get rid of it. I have it very badly."

"Come, order, order – the tale; let's hear the end of that, since it has begun."

"With all my heart. Come, neighbor."

"Well, as I said, he was fidgety, but yet he was not a man to be very easily frightened or overcome, for he was stout and bold.

When he shut himself up in the room, he took out a bottle of some good wine and helped himself to drink; it was good old wine, and he soon felt himself warmed and comforted. He could have faced the enemy.

"If one bottle produces such an effect," he muttered, "what will two do?"

This was a question that could only be solved by trying it, and this he proceeded to do.

But first he drew a brace of long barreled pistols from his coat pocket, and taking a powder-flask and bullets from his pocket also, he loaded them very carefully.

"There," said he, "are my bull-dogs, and rare watch-dogs they are. They never bark but they bite. Now, if anybody does come, it will be all up with them. Tricks upon travelers ain't a safe game when I have these, and now for the other bottle."

He opened the other bottle, and thought, if anything, it was better than the first. He drank it rather quickly, to be sure, and then he began to feel sleepy and tired.

"I think I shall go to bed," he said; "that is, if I can find my way there, for it does seem to me as if the door was travelling. Never mind, it will make a call here again presently, and then I'll get through."

So saying, he arose. Taking the candle in his hand, he walked with a better step than might have been expected under the circumstance. True, the candle wagged to and fro, and his shadow danced upon the wall, but still, when he got to the bed, he secured his door, put the light in a safe place, threw himself down, and was fast asleep in a few moments; or rather he fell into a doze instantaneously.

How long he remained in this state he knew not, but he was suddenly awakened by a loud bang as though something heavy had fallen flat upon the floor – such, for instance, as a door, or anything of that sort. He jumped up, rubbed his eyes, and could even then hear the reverberations through the house.

"What is that?" he muttered; "what is that?"

He listened, and thought he could hear something moving downstairs, and for a moment he was seized with worry, but remembering, I suppose, that there were some valuables downstairs that were worth fighting for, he carefully extinguished the light that still burned and crept quietly down the stairs.

When he got downstairs, he thought he could hear someone scramble up the kitchen stairs and into the room where the bureau was. Listening for a moment to ascertain if there were more than one, and then feeling convinced there was not, he followed into the parlor, where he heard the cabinet open by a key.

This was a new miracle, and one he could not understand, and then he heard the papers begin to rattle and rustle; so, drawing out one of the pistols, he cocked it, and walked in.

The figure instantly began to jump about; it was dressed in white – in grave-clothes. He was terribly nervous, and he shook so badly he feared to fire the pistol, but at length he did, and the report was followed by a fall and a loud groan.

This was very dreadful – very dreadful, but all was quiet, and he lit the candle again, and approached the body to examine it and ascertain if he knew who it was. A groan came from it. The bureau was open, and the figure firmly clutched a will in his hand.

The figure was dressed in grave-clothes, and he started up when he saw the form and features of his own uncle, the man who was dead, who somehow or other had escaped his confinement and found his way up here. He held his will firmly, and the nephew was so horrified and stunned that he threw down the light, and rushed out of the room with a shout of terror and never returned. The narrator concluded, and one of the guests said, "And do you really believe it?"

"No, no – to be sure not."

"It was now half-past twelve and, as Tom Eccles had not come back and the landlord did not feel disposed to draw any more liquor, they left the inn and retired to their separate houses in a great state of anxiety to know the fate of their respective wagers.

Chapter 64
The Vampire in the Moonlight – The False Friend

Having traveled part of the distance from the town to the old ruins, Tom Eccles began to feel that what he had undertaken was not perhaps such child's-play as he had at first imagined it to be. Somehow or another he began remembering all the stories, and the long-since-forgotten tales of superstition that he had learned in early childhood. They came back upon him, suggesting to his mind a thousand uncomfortable fancies of the strangest description.

No doubt if he had he turned around and headed back to the inn again instead of continuing towards the old ruins, he would soon have shaken off these "thick-coming fancies;" but such a result was not to be expected, so long as he kept on toward the dismal place he had pledged himself to reach.

As he crossed meadow after meadow, he began to ask himself some questions, which he found that he could not exactly answer in a manner that he could find consoling under the present state of things.

Among these questions that he could not answer the most important one was: "It's no argument against vampyres because I don't see the use of 'em – is it?" This he was compelled to answer honestly once he had raised it, and his answer was not comforting, especially when, in addition, he began to remember that without the shadow of a doubt Sir Francis Varney, the supposed vampyre, had been chased across the fields to that very ruin where he had then disappeared and remained unfound despite the best efforts of many searchers to discover him. This memory made him decidedly uncomfortable, and he now found himself in a most unpromising situation.

"No," he said, "no. Hang it, I won't go back now to be made the laughing-stock of the whole town, which I should be. Come what may of it, I will go on as I have commenced; I shall put on as stout a heart as I can."

Having come to this resolve, he strove to banish from his mind those disagreeable reminiscences that had been oppressing him and turned his attention to subjects of a different nature; how he might spend his winnings from the wagers.

Soon thereafter he came within sight of the ruins. Then he slackened his pace a little, telling himself, with a pardonable self-deceit,

The Flight Of The Vampyre

that it was common, ordinary caution causing him to slow his steps, nothing at all in the shape of fear.

"Time enough," he remarked, "to be afraid when I see anything to be afraid of, which I don't see as yet. So, as all's right, I may as well put a good face upon the matter."

He tried to whistle a tune, but it turned out only a melancholy failure; so he gave that up in despair and walked on until he got within a hundred yards, or thereabouts, of the old ruins.

He thus proceeded, then stopped to hold his ear close to the ground; he listened attentively for several minutes. Somehow, he fancied that a strange, murmuring sound came to his ears, but he was not quite sure that it proceeded from the ruins because it was just that sort of sound that might come from a long way off, being mellowed by distance, although, perhaps, loud enough at its source.

"Well, well," he whispered to himself, "it don't matter much, after all. I must go ahead and hide the handkerchiefs somewhere, or else be laughed at besides losing my wagers. The former I don't like, and the latter I cannot afford."

Thus clinching the matter by such compelling arguments, he walked on until he was almost within the very shadow of the ruins, and it was at this juncture that his footsteps may have been heard by Marchdale and Sir Francis Varney.

Then he paused again, but all was profoundly quiet. He began to think that the strange sort of murmuring noise that he had heard must have come from far off, and not at all from any person or persons within the ruins.

"Let me see," he said to himself; "I have five handkerchiefs to hide among the old ruins somewhere, and the sooner I do so the better, because then I will get away, for, as regards staying here to watch, upon second thoughts, I don't intend to do it, for no one in the village could know the difference, and second thoughts, they say, are generally best."

With the most careful footsteps now, as if he were treading upon some fragile substance which he feared to injure, he advanced until he was within the shadow of the ancient place which now bore so ill a reputation.

He then made to himself much the same remark that Sir Francis Varney had made to Marchdale with respect to the brightening up of the sky as the moon rose upon the horizon, and he saw more clearly around him, although he could not find any good place to hide the handkerchiefs.

"I must and will," he said, "hide them securely, for it would be remarkably unpleasant after coming here and winning my wagers, to have the proofs that I had done so taken away by some chance visitor to the place."

He at length saw a tolerably large stone, standing slanted against one of the walls. Its size attracted him. He thought to himself that if his strength was sufficient to move it, that it would be a good thing to do so, and to place the handkerchiefs beneath it. For at all events, it was so heavy that it could not be kicked aside, and no one without some sort of motive to do so, beyond the mere love of labor, would set about moving it from its position.

"I may search further and fare worse," he said to himself; "so here shall all the handkerchiefs lie, to afford a proof that I have been here."

He packed them into a small mass, and then stooped to roll aside the heavy stone. Then, at the moment, before he could apply his strength to that purpose, he heard someone in his immediate neighborhood, say, "Hist!"

This was so sudden and so utterly unexpected that he not only ceased his exertions to move the stone, but he nearly fell down in his surprise.

"Hist – hist!" sounded again.

"What – what," gasped Tom Eccles – "what are you?"

The sound then changed tone, to, "Hush – hush – hush!"

The perspiration broke out upon his brow, and he leaned against the wall for support, as he managed to say, faintly, "Well, hush – what then?"

"Hist!"

"Well, I hear you. Where are you?" he cried increasing in anger and fear.

"Near at hand. Who are you?"

"Tom Eccles," he answered, happy at the thought that this was not a spirit, since spirits generally didn't carry on conversations – or so he had been lead by the stories of his youth to believe. He asked, "Who are you?"

"A friend. Have you seen anything?"

"No; I wish I could. I should like to see you if I could."

"I'm coming," the voice stated, and there was a slow and cautious footstep, and Marchdale advanced to where Tom Eccles was standing.

"Come, now," said the latter, when he saw the dusky-looking form stalking towards him; "till I know you better, I'll be obliged to you to keep off. I am well armed. Keep your distance, be you friend or foe."

"Armed!" exclaimed Marchdale, and he at once paused, having a dislike of being on the wrong end of a bullet.

"Yes, I am."

"But I am a friend. I have no objection to telling you my errand. I am a friend of the Bannerworth family, and have kept watch here now for two nights in the hopes of meeting with Varney, the vampyre."

"The devil you have! And pray what may your name be?"

"Marchdale."

"If you be Mr. Marchdale, I know you by sight, for I have seen you with Mr. Henry Bannerworth several times. Come out from among the shadows and let us have a look at you, but, till you do, don't come within arm's length of me. I am not naturally suspicious, but we cannot be too careful."

"Oh! Certainly – certainly. The silver edge of the moon is now just peeping up from the east, and you will be able to see me quite well if you step away from the shadow of the wall by which you now are standing."

This was a reasonable enough proposition, and Tom Eccles at once acceded to it by stepping out boldly into the partial moonlight which now began to fall upon the open meadows, tinting the grass with a silvery light and rendering even minute objects visible. The moment he saw Marchdale he knew him and, advancing frankly to him, he said, "I know you, sir, well."

"And what brings you here?"

"A wager for one thing, and a wish to see the vampyre for another."

"Indeed!" Marchdale exclaimed in accents of surprise.

"Yes, I must confess I have such a wish, along with a still stronger one of capturing him, if possible, and as there are now two of us, why may we not do it?"

"As for capturing him," said Marchdale, "I should prefer shooting him."

"You would?"

"I would, indeed. I have seen him once shot down, and he is now, I have no doubt, as well as ever. What were you doing with that huge stone I saw you bending over?"

"I have some handkerchiefs to hide here, as a proof that I have really been to this place tonight."

"Oh, I will show you a better spot, where there is a crevice in which you can place them with perfect safety. Will you walk with me into the ruins?"

Tom Eccles readily agreed to this proposition, and the two men moved deeper into the shadowy ruins.

"It's odd enough," remarked Marchdale, after he had shown Tom Eccles where to hide the handkerchiefs, "that you and I should both be here upon so similar an errand."

"I'm very glad of it. It robs the place of its gloom, and makes it ten times more endurable than it otherwise would be. What do you propose to do if you see the vampyre?"

"I shall try a pistol bullet on him. You say you are armed?"

"Yes."

"With pistols?"

"One. Here it is."

"A huge weapon; loaded well, of course?"

"Oh, yes, I can depend upon it, but I did not intend to use it, unless I was assailed."

"'Tis well." Marchale said before starting suddenly and looking around, "What is that?"

"What – what?"

"Don't you see anything there? Come farther back. Look – look. At the corner of that wall there; I am certain there is the flutter of a human garment."

"There is – there is."

"Hush! Keep close. It must be the vampyre."

"Give me my pistol. What are you doing with it?"

"Only ramming the charge more firmly for you. Take it. If that is Varney the vampyre, I shall challenge him to surrender the moment he appears, and if he does not, I will fire upon him, and you do likewise."

"Well, I – I don't know," Eccles said.

"You have scruples about shooting the vampyre?"

"I certainly have; he ain't done nothing to me personally."

The Flight Of The Vampyre

"Well, well – don't you fire, then, but leave it to me. There; look – look. Now have you any doubt? There he goes, in his cloak. It is – it is… "

"Varney, by Heavens!" cried Tom Eccles.

"Surrender!" shouted Marchdale.

At that instant, Sir Francis Varney sprang forward and made off at a rapid pace across the meadows.

"Fire after him – fire!" cried Marchdale, "or he will escape. My pistol has missed fire. He will be off."

On the impulse of the moment, and thus urged by the voice and the gesture of his companion, Tom Eccles took aim as well as he could and fired after the retreating form of Sir Francis Varney. His conscience smote him as he heard the report and saw the flash of the large pistol amid the half-darkness that was still around.

The effect of the shot was then painfully apparent to him. He saw Varney stop instantly; then make a vain attempt to stagger forward a little, and finally fall heavily to the earth with all the appearance of one killed upon the spot.

"You have hit him," said Marchdale – "you have hit him. Bravo!"

"I have – hit him," echoed Eccles faintly.

"Yes, a capital shot, by Jove!"

"I am very sorry."

"Sorry! Sorry for ridding the world of such a being! What was in your pistol?"

"A couple of slugs."

"Well, they have taken a lodging in him, that's quite clear. Let's go up and finish him at once."

"He seems finished," observed Eccles.

"I beg your pardon. When the moonbeams fall upon him, he'll get up and walk away as if nothing was the matter."

"Will he?" cried Tom with animation. "Will he?"

"Certainly he will."

"Thank God for that. Now, hark you, Mr. Marchdale: I should not have fired if you had not at the moment urged me to do so. Now, I shall stay and see if the effect which you talk of will ensue, and although it may convince me that he is a vampyre, and that there are such things, he may go off, scot free for all I shall do to prevent it."

"Go off?"

"Yes; I don't want to have even a vampyre's blood upon my hands."

"You are exceedingly delicate."

"Perhaps I am; it's my way, though. I have shot him – not you, mind; so, in a manner of speaking, he belongs to me. Now, mark you: I won't have him touched any more tonight, unless you think there's a chance of making a prisoner of him without violence."

"There he lies; you can go and make a prisoner of him at once, dead as he is, and if you take him out of the moonlight…"

"I understand; he won't recover."

"Certainly not."

"But, as I want him to recover, that don't suit me."

"Well, I cannot but honor your scruples, although I do not actually share in them, but I promise you that since such is your wish, I will take no steps against the vampyre, but let us come up to him and see if he is really dead, or only badly wounded."

Tom Eccles hung back a little from this proposal, but upon being urged again by Marchdale and told that he need get no closer than he chose, he consented, and the two of them approached the prostrate form of Sir Francis Varney, which lay upon its face in the faint moonlight which each moment was gathering strength and power.

"He lies upon his face," said Marchdale. "Will you go and turn him over?"

"Who? I? God forbid I should touch him."

"Well – well, I will. Come on."

They halted within a couple of yards of the body. Tom Eccles would not go a step farther; so Marchdale advanced alone, and pretended to be, with great repugnance, examining for the wound.

"He is quite dead," he said; "but I cannot see the wound."

"I think he turned his head as I fired."

"Did he? Let us see."

Marchdale lifted up the head and disclosed such a mass of clotted-looking blood that Tom Eccles at once took to his heels. He did not stop until he was nearly as far off as the ruins. Marchdale followed him more slowly, and when he came up to him he said, "The slugs have taken effect on his face."

"I know it – I know it. Don't tell me."

"He looks horrible."

"And I am a murderer."

The Flight Of The Vampyre

"Psha! You look upon this matter too seriously. Think who and what he was, and then you will soon acquit yourself of being open to any such charge."

"I am bewildered, Mr. Marchdale, and cannot now know whether he is a vampyre or not. If he is not a vampyre, I have murdered, most unjustifiably, a fellow-creature."

"Well, what if he is?"

"Why, even then I do not know but that I ought to consider myself every bit as guilty. He is one of God's creatures, even if he were ten times a vampyre."

"Well, you really do take a serious view of the affair."

"Not more serious than it deserves."

"And what do you mean to do?"

"I shall remain here to await the result of what you tell me will ensue if he is really a vampire. Even now the moonbeams are full upon him, and each moment increasing in intensity. Do you think you he will recover?"

"I do indeed."

"Then I will wait here to observe it."

"Since that is your resolve, I will keep you company. We shall easily find some old stone in the ruins which will serve us for a seat, and there, at leisure, we can keep our eyes upon the dead body, and be able to observe if it make the least movement."

This plan was adopted, and they sat down just within the ruins, but in such a place that they had a full view of the dead body as it appeared to be, of Sir Francis Varney, upon which the sweet moonbeams shone full and clear.

Tom Eccles related how he was incited to come upon his expedition, but he might have spared himself that trouble, as Marchdale had been in a secluded corner of the inn parlor before he came to his appointment with Varney, and heard the business for the most part proposed.

Half-an-hour, certainly not more, might have elapsed when suddenly Tom Eccles uttered an exclamation, partly of surprise and partly of terror, "He moves; he moves!" he cried. "Look at the vampyre's body."

Marchdale affected to look with an all-absorbing interest, and there was Sir Francis Varney, slowly raising one arm with the hand outstretched towards the moon, as if invoking that luminary to shed more of its beams upon him. Then the body moved slowly, like someone writhing in pain, and yet unable to move from the spot on which it lay. From the head to the foot, the whole frame seemed to be convulsed, and now and then as the ghastly object seemed to be gathering more strength, the limbs were thrown out with a rapid and a frightful looking violence.

It was truly a frightful sight to see and, although Marchdale, of course, tolerably well preserved his equanimity, only now and then and for appearances sake affecting to be wonderfully shocked, poor Tom Eccles was in such a state of horror and fright that he could not, if he would, have flown from the spot, so fascinated was he by the horrible spectacle.

This was a state of things which continued for many minutes, and then the body showed evident symptoms of so much returning animation, that it was about to rise from its gory bed and mingle once again with the living.

"Behold!" exclaimed Marchdale, "behold!"

"Heaven have mercy upon us!"

"It is as I said; the beams of the moon have revived the vampyre. You perceive now that there can be no doubt that Varney is a vampyre?"

"Yes, yes, I see him; I see him," uttered Eccles in tones in which mingled amazement and hysteria.

Sir Francis Varney now, as if with a great struggle rose to his feet, and looked up at the bright moon for some moments with such an air and manner that it would not have required any very great amount of imagination to conceive that he was returning to it some sort of thanksgiving for the good that it had done to him.

He then seemed for some moments in a state of considerable indecision as to which way he should proceed. He turned around several times. Then he advanced a step or two towards the house, but apparently his resolution changed again, and casting his eyes upon the ruins, he at once made towards them.

This was too much for the courage of Tom Eccles. It was all very well to look on at some distance and observe the wonderful and inexplicable proceedings of the vampyre, but when he showed symptoms of making a nearer acquaintance, it was not to be borne.

"Why, he's coming here," moaned Tom.

"He does seem to be headed this way," remarked Marchdale.

"Do you mean to stay?"

"I think I shall. I should very much like to question him, and as we are two to one, I really think we can have nothing to fear."

"Do you? I'm altogether of a different opinion. A man who has more lives than a cat don't much mind at what odds he fights. You may stay if you like."

"You do not mean to say that you will desert me?"

"I don't see as how you can call it deserting you; if we had come out together on this adventure, I would have stayed it out with you, but as we came separate and independent, we may as well go back so."

"Well, but... "

"Good morning," cried Tom, and he at once took to his heels towards the town, without staying to pay any attention to the remonstrance's of Marchdale, who called after him in vain.

"Is he much terrified?" Varney asked as he came up to Marchdale.

"Yes, most completely; we shan't see him again this night."

"This, then, will make a good story in the town."

"It will, indeed, and it will do more than a little to enhance your reputation."

"Well, well; it don't much matter now, but if by terrifying people I can purchase for myself anything like immunity for the past, I shall be satisfied."

"I think you may now safely reckon that you have done so. This man who has fled with so much precipitation, had courage, or else he would have shrunk from coming here at all."

"True, but his courage and his presence here arose from his strong doubts as to the existence of such beings as vampyres."

"Yes, and now that he is convinced in the reality of such beings, his bravery has evaporated along with his doubts; and such a tale as he has now to tell will be found sufficient to convert even the most skeptical in the town."

"I hope so."

"And yet it cannot much avail you."

"Not personally, but I must confess that I am not dead to all human passions, and I feel some desire of revenge against those dastards who by hundreds have hunted me, burnt down my house, and sought my destruction."

"That is only normal."

"I would fain leave among them a legacy of fear. Such fear as shall haunt them and their children for years to come. I would wish that the name of Varney, the vampire, should be a sound of terror for generations."

"It will be so," Marchdale stated dryly, before continuing, "And now, then, for a consideration of what is to be done with our prisoner. What is your resolve upon that point?"

"I have considered it while I was lying upon yon green grass waiting for the friendly moonbeams to fall upon my face, and it seems to me that there is no sort of resource but to…"

"Kill him?"

"No, no."

"What then?"

"To set him free."

"Nay! Have you considered the immense hazard of doing so? Think again; I pray you think again. I am decidedly of the opinion that he more than suspects who are his enemies, and in that case you know what consequences would ensue, especially for me; besides, have we not enough already to encounter? Why should we add another young, bold, determined spirit to the band which is already arrayed against us?"

"You talk in vain, Marchdale; I know to what it all tends; you have a strong desire for the death of this young man."

"No; there you wrong me. I have no desire for his death, for its own sake, but where great interests are at stake, there must be sacrifices made."

"So there must; therefore, I will make a sacrifice and let this young prisoner free from his dungeon."

"If such is your determination, I know quite well it is useless to quarrel with you over it. When do you propose giving him his freedom?"

"I will not act incautiously, I promise you. I will attempt to get from him some promise that he will not be an active instrument against me. Perchance since Bannerworth Hall which he will be sure to visit wears such an air of desertion, I may be able to persuade him that both the Bannerworth family and his uncle have left this part of the country; so that, without making any inquiry for them about the neighborhood, he may be induced to leave at once."

"That would be well."

"Good; your prudence approves of the plan, and therefore it shall be done."

"I am rather inclined to think" said Marchdale, with a slight tone of sarcasm, "that if my prudence did not approve of the plan, it would still be done."

"Most probably," Varney said calmly.

"Will you release him tonight?"

"It is morning, now. I do not think I will release him till sunset. Has he provision to last him until then?"

"He has."

"Well, then, two hours after sunset I will come here and release him from his weary bondage, and now I must go to find some place in which to hide. As for Bannerworth Hall, I will yet have it in my power; I have sworn to do so, I will keep my oath."

"The accomplishment of our purpose, I regret to say, seems as far off as ever."

"Not so… not so. As I before remarked, we must disappear for a time only to lull suspicion. There will then arise a period when Bannerworth Hall will neither be watched, as it is now, nor will it be inhabited. There will be a period before the Bannerworth family has made up its mind to go back to it, and when long watching without a result has become too tiresome to be continued at all; then we can at once pursue our object."

"Be it so."

"And now, Marchdale, I want more money."

"More money!"

"Yes; you know that I have had large demands of late."

"But I certainly had an impression that you were possessed, by the death of someone, with very ample means."

"Yes, but there is a means by which all I get is taken from me. I have no real resources that are not being rapidly used up, so I must come upon you again."

"I have already completely crippled myself as regards money matters in this enterprise, and I do certainly hope that the fruits will not be far distant. If they are much longer delayed, I shall really not know what to do. However, come to the lodge where you have been staying, and then I will give you, to the extent of my ability, whatever sum you think your present needs require."

"Come on, then, at once. I would certainly rather leave this placed now, before daybreak. Come on, I say, come on."

Sir Francis Varney and Marchdale walked for some time as silent companions across the meadows. It was evident that there was not between these associates the very best of feelings. Marchdale was always annoyed at the aura of authority over him held by Sir Francis Varney, while the latter scarcely cared to conceal any portion of the contempt with which he regarded his hypocritical companion.

Some very strong band of union must surely bind these two strange persons together! It must be something of a more than common nature which induces Marchdale not only to obey the behests of his mysterious companion, but to supply him so readily with money as we perceive he promises to do.

And as regards Varney, the vampyre, he also must have some great object in view to induce him to run such a world of risk, and to take so much trouble as he was doing with the Bannerworth family.

What his object is, and what is the object of Marchdale, will, now that we have progressed so far in our story, soon appear, and then much that is perfectly inexplicable will become clear and distinct, and we shall find that some strong human motives are at the bottom of it all.

Chapter 65
Varney's Visit to the Dungeon of the Lonely Prisoner in the Ruins

It was evident that Marchdale was not nearly so scrupulous as Sir Francis Varney in what he chose to do. He would, without hesitation, have sacrificed the life of that prisoner in the lonely dungeon, whom it would be an insult to the understanding of our readers, not to presume that they had, long before this, established in their minds to be Charles Holland.

His own safety seemed to be the paramount consideration with Marchdale, and it was evident that he cared for nothing in comparison with that desire for safety.

It says much, however, for Sir Francis Varney, that he did not give in to such a blood-thirsty feeling, but rather chose to set the prisoner free and run all the chances of the danger to which he might expose himself by such a course of conduct, rather than insuring his own safety by the murder of the prisoner.

Sir Francis Varney is evidently a character of strangely mixed feelings. It is quite evident that he has some great goal which he wishes to accomplish at almost any risk to himself, but it is equally evident at the same time, that he wishes to accomplish it with the least possible injury to others, or else he would never have behaved as he had during his interview with the beautiful and persecuted Flora Bannerworth, nor would he now have suggested the idea of setting Charles Holland free from the dreary dungeon in which he had, for so long, been confined.

We are always anxious and willing to give everyone credit for the good that is in them, and hence we are pleased to find that Sir Francis Varney, the vampyre, despite his singular status and capabilities, has something sufficiently human about his mind and feelings to induce him to do as little injury as possible to others in the pursuit of his own goals.

Of the two, vampyre as he is, we prefer him over the despicable and hypocritical Marchdale, who, under the pretence of being the friend of the Bannerworth family, would freely have inflicted upon them the most deadly injuries.

It was quite clear that he was dreadfully disappointed that Sir Francis Varney would not permit him to murder Charles Holland, and it was with a gloomy and dissatisfied air that he left the ruins and proceeded towards the town, after what we may almost term the altercation he had had with Varney, the vampyre, upon that subject.

It must not be supposed that Sir Francis Varney, however, was blind to the danger which must inevitably accrue from permitting Charles Holland his freedom.

What the latter would be able to state would be more than sufficient to convince the Bannerworths that something was going on which, however supernatural as it might seem to be, still seemed to have some human and ordinary objects for its ends.

Sir Francis Varney thought over all this before he proceeded, according to his promise, to the dungeon of the prisoner, but it would seem as if there was considerable difficulty in arriving at any satisfactory means for making Charles Holland's release less dangerous to himself than it would be likely to be, if, unfettered by obligation, Charles Holland was at once set free.

The Flight Of The Vampyre

At the solemn hour of midnight on the night following the one on which he had held the interview with Marchdale, Sir Francis Varney alone sought the silent ruins. He was attired, as usual, in his huge cloak and, indeed, the chilly air of the evening warranted such protection against its numerous discomforts.

Had anyone seen him creeping about that evening, they would have observed an air of great doubt and irresolution upon his brow, as if he were struggling with some impulses which he found it extremely difficult to restrain.

"I know very well," he muttered as he walked among the shadow of the ruins, "that Marchdale's reasoning is coldly and horribly correct when he says that there is danger in setting this youth free, but I am about to leave this place and not show myself for some time, and I cannot reconcile myself to inflicting upon him the horror of a death by starvation which is what must happen if I fail to let him free."

It was a night of more than usual dullness, and as Sir Francis Varney removed the mossy stone which hid the narrow entrance to the dungeons, a chilly feeling crept over him, and he could not help wondering if Marchdale might have played him false and neglected to supply the prisoner food, according to his promise.

Hastily he descended to the dungeons far less cautiously than he usually did. He proceeded onwards until he reached that particular dungeon in which our young friend had been so long confined.

"Speak," said Sir Francis Varney, as he entered the dungeon. "If the occupant of this dread place lives, let him answer one who is as much his friend as he has been his enemy."

"I have no friend," Charles Holland said faintly; "unless it is someone who would come and set me free."

"And how do you know that I am not here to do so?"

"Your voice sounds like that of one of my persecutors. Why do you not just take me life? I should be better pleased that you would do so than that I should be forced to wear out the useless struggles of existence in such a dreary and wretched abode as this."

"Young man," said Sir Francis Varney, "I have come to you on a greater errand of mercy than, probably, you will ever give me credit for. There is one who would too readily have granted your present request, and who would at once have taken that life with which you profess to be so wearied, but which may yet present to you some of its sunniest and most beautiful aspects."

"Your tones are friendly," said Charles; "yet I dread some new deception. I know that you are one of those who consigned me by stratagem and brute force to this place, and therefore any good that may be promised by you presents itself to me in a very doubtful character."

"I cannot be surprised," said Sir Francis Varney, "at such sentiments arising from your lips; nevertheless, I am inclined to save you. You have been detained here because it was supposed that by your being held, a particular object would be best obtained by your absence. That object, however, has failed, and I do not feel further inclined to protract your sufferings. Have you any guess as to the parties who have thus confined you?"

"I am unaccustomed to dissembling and, therefore, I will say at once that I have a guess."

"In what way does it tend?"

"Against Sir Francis Varney, called the vampyre."

"Does it strike you that this may be a dangerous candor?" – "It may, or it may not be; I cannot help it. I know I am at the mercy of my foes, and I do not believe that anything I can say or do will make my situation worse or better."

"You are much mistaken there. In other hands than mine, it might make it much worse, but it happens to be one of my weaknesses that I am charged with candor, and that I admire boldness of disposition."

"Indeed! And yet can behave in the manner you have done towards me."

"Yes. There are more things in heaven and earth than are dreamt of in your philosophy. I am more inclined to set you free because if I procure from you a promise, which I intend to attempt, I am inclined to believe that you will keep it."

"I shall assuredly keep whatever promise I may make. Tell me your conditions, and if they be such as honor and honesty will permit me to accede to, I will do so willingly and at once. Heaven knows I am weary enough of this miserable imprisonment."

"Will you promise me then, if I set you free, not to mention your suspicions that it is to Sir Francis Varney you owe this ill turn, and not to attempt any act of revenge against him as retaliation for it."

"I cannot promise so much as that. Freedom would be a poor boon if I were not permitted to freely converse about some of the circumstances connected with my captivity."

The Flight Of The Vampyre

"You object, then, to my conditions?"

"I do to the former of your propositions, but not to the latter. I will promise not to go at all out of my way to execute any vengeance upon you, but I will not promise that I will not communicate the circumstances of my forced absence from them to those friends whose opinion I so much value."

Sir Francis Varney was silent for a few moments, and then he said, in a tone of deep solemnity, "There are ninety-nine persons out of a hundred who would take your life for the independence of your tongue, but I am as the hundredth one, who looks with a benevolent eye at your proceedings. Will you promise me, if I remove the fetters which now bind your limbs, that you will make no personal attack upon me, for I am weary of personal contention, and I will have no disposition to endure it. Will you make me this promise?"

"I will so promise."

Without another word, but trusting implicitly to the promise which had been given to him, Sir Francis Varney produced a small key from his pocket and used it to unlock the padlock which confined the chains about the prisoner.

Charles Holland was then enabled to shake them off, and then for the first time in some weeks, he rose to his feet, and felt all the exquisite relief of being comparatively free from bondage.

"This is delightful indeed," he said.

"It is," agreed Sir Francis Varney, "it is but a foretaste of the happiness you will enjoy when you are entirely free. You see that I have trusted you."

"You have trusted me as you might trust me, and you perceive that I have kept my word."

"You have, and since you decline to make me the promise which I would wish to have from you, to the effect that you would not mention me as one of the authors of your calamity, I must trust to your honor not to attempt revenge for what you have suffered."

"As I said, that I will freely promise. There can be but little difficulty to any generous mind in giving up such a feeling. In consequence of your sparing me what you might still have inflicted, I will let the past rest as if it had never happened really to me, and speak of it to others but as a circumstance which I wish not to refer to, and prefer should be buried in oblivion."

"It is well, and now I have a request to make of you, which, perhaps, you will consider the hardest of all."

"Name it. I feel myself bound to a considerable extent to comply with whatever you may demand of me that is not contrary to honorable principle."

"Then it is this, that, comparatively free as you are, and in a condition as you are to assert your own freedom, you will not do so hastily, or for a considerable period; in fact, I wish and expect that you should wait yet awhile, until it shall suit me to say that it is my pleasure that you shall be free."

"That is, indeed, a hard condition to a man who feels, as you yourself remark that he can assert his freedom. It is one which I have still a hope you will not persevere in."

"Nay, young man, I think that I have treated you with enough generosity in setting you free instead of killing you to make you feel that I am not the worst of foes you could have had. All I require of you is that you should wait here for about an hour. It is now nearly one o'clock; will you wait until you hear it strike two before you actually make movement to leave this place?"

Charles Holland hesitated for some moments, and then he grudged, "Do not fancy that I am not one who appreciates the singular trust you have reposed in me, and however repugnant to me it may be to remain here, a voluntary prisoner, I am inclined to do so, if it be but to convince you that the trust you have reposed in me is not in vain, and that I can behave with equal generosity to you as you can to me."

"Be it so," said Sir Francis Varney; "I shall leave you with a full reliance that you will keep your word, and now, farewell. When you think of me, fancy me a person rather unfortunate than criminal, and tell yourself that even Varney, the vampyre, had some traits in his character which although they might not raise your esteem, at all events did not loudly call for your reprobation."

"I shall do so. Oh! Flora, Flora, I shall look upon you once again, after believing and thinking that I had bidden you a long and last adieu. My own beautiful Flora, it is joy indeed to think that I shall look upon that face again, which, to my perception is full of all the majesty of loveliness."

Sir Francis Varney looked coldly on Charles while he uttered this enthusiastic speech.

"Remember," he said, "till two o'clock;" and he walked towards the door of the dungeon. "You will have no difficulty in finding your way out of this place. Doubtless you already perceive the entrance by which I gained admission."

"Had I been free," said Charles, "and had the use of my limbs, I should long before this have worked my way to life and liberty."

"'Tis well. Good night."

Varney walked from the place, and closed the door behind him, not replacing the stone which prior to this had always blocked the entrance and the light. With a slow and stately step he left the ruins, and Charles Holland found himself once more alone, but in a much more enviable condition than he would have for many weeks called his own. He was now free.

Endnotes

---

[i] Varney, the vampire, does not die until the end of book five, so this is a bit early to mention his death.

[ii] There are no chapters 41 – 43. They are missing on the original manuscripts; it can be assumed that this is a publishing error since thstory resumes from book one at the correct point.

[iii] Prig: A prissy looking man who believes he is better than everyone else.

[iv] Obdurate: Stubborn

[v] Immolate: to burn someone alive (in this case – undead!).

[vi] Beadle: A minor Church official who acts as an usher during Church services.

[vii] Ranter: A Ranter was an individual who spent his time in loud exhortations – usually towards moral behavior.

[viii] Chapel of Little Bozzelhum: A nonsense name for a non-Anglican Church.

[ix] Horse Marine: A marine mounted on horseback or a cavalry-man doing duty on board ship.

[x] Marines: A class of naval troops that serve both on land, and at sea. The land part is the insult when either Jack Pringle of the Admiral use the term.

[xi] Lubber: an awkward unskilled sailor.

[xii] Dragoons: A body of soldiers trained primarily to fight on foot, but also trained in cavalry combat.

[xiii] Lumber-rooms: Attics or storage rooms for all the excess stuff accumulated.

[xiv] Checkstring: A string pulled by one within the coach to communicate instructions to the driver.

[xv] Holland: A type of alcoholic beverage.

[xvi] Boatswain: An officer on a ship who is mid-level, controlling the work of the non-commissioned officers. He blows a whistle to signal what type of work they are to do.

[xvii] Holland: A type of alcoholic beverage.

[xviii] Temperance: Giving up liquor.

[xix] Gammon: Spoken nonsense meant to fool someone into a false belief.

[xx] Wits and men of spirit: The cool crowd, you know, the ones who live to party.

Upcoming From Scion Press

Risen From The Grave: Varney the Vampyre Book One: The Feast Of Blood. (September 2009)

Flora screamed as the vampire dragged her across the bed by her hair. If she had known it was a vampire tapping at her window, Flora Bannerworth would have screamed earlier. But the violence of the storm outside fooled her into thinking it was just a branch. But branches don't feast on blood. This vampire wants more than blood.

Thus begins James Malcom Rymer's *Varney The Vampyre Book One: The Feast Of The Blood,* raising questions about Flora's future: married or spinster, human or vampire? Will her fiancé love her enough to overlook her possible destiny? Who will she choose; vampire or fiancé? And who will save her from this fate which is not only worse than death, but beyond death?

This modern language version, *Risen From The Grave,* produced by Leslie Ormandy allows a modern reader a glimpse of an earlier era, and their ideas of Vampires.